Only Billionaires Can Play

Fred Leavitt

Published by Open Books

Interior Design by Siva Ram Maganti

Cover image © Nadia Grapes shutterstock.com/g/Nadezda+Grapes

ISBN-13: 978-1948598538

Any resemblance between most of the characters in this book and real people is accidental. Colombo is real—and unhappy that I've given him a minor role. If first novels are autobiographical, then Paul is the stand-in for me. But if the two of us stood side by side, nobody would have trouble telling us apart. Paul is better-looking, smarter, more athletic, and a more decent person. Marice, with a few minor changes, is my wife Diane.

PART I

Paul Combes: Life Was Simple Then

Paul Combes ripped April, 1994 from the calendar and fixed a cold gaze on May. The cartoon pig-man with vaguely Paulish features stared back through heavily lidded eyes. Splayed in belly-down position, baseball in mouth and catcher's mitt on left paw, pig-man watched dejectedly as opposing runners sped around the basepaths. Months earlier, Paul had paid his friend in the art department to draw the caricature. Wasted money. He needed no added incentive to shape up for the July softball game pitting his radio station KDJM against KSMO. Losers treated winners to dinner, and KDJM had footed the bill for seven years straight.

Paul dropped for fifty pushups, swallowed creatine stirred in water, waited ten minutes, tried for fifty more. Bad left shoulder searing with pain, he managed forty-two before collapsing on the exercise mat. He rolled onto his back and stared at the 3 x 5 index card tacked to the wall next to pig-man. The taunting message bore his scrawl: "Too low they build who build beneath the stars." Edward Young.

Still on his back, he did fifty sit-ups and a round of stretching, then rolled over again for another dozen pushups. Breathing hard, he addressed pig-man. "I'll do two sets of fifty tomorrow, two seventy-fives the next day, three sets within two weeks." He intended to be in peak condition by July 4.

Station manager Arlene Conant joined Paul in the cafeteria line.

She'd been on a week's vacation, and something seemed subtly different. Hair? Clothing? Weight? He said, "That's a pretty blouse." Arlene nodded and took a tuna salad for her tray, her tepid response making clear that he'd paid the wrong compliment. Paul built a giant pyramid of food and inched it along the checkout counter, careful not to tumble mashed potatoes into sole fillets or fruit salad. The homeless man outside rejected obvious leftovers. He tried estimating the volume of the food pile but couldn't recall the formula for volume of a pyramid. Anyway, more than he could eat at one sitting. Arlene muttered, "Where do you put it all? That's enough to feed a football team."

Leaning toward the recently hired cashier, Paul nodded to indicate a significantly overweight man further down the line. He whispered, "You probably recognize Gordy Jackson. Best DJ in the country, but touchy about his girth. Gordy hates for people to see how much he eats, so he puts just a little on his tray and I pick up the rest. He'll pay for this." Arlene chuckled and the cashier joined in, willing co-conspirator. The two patrons sat near the cash register and a few seconds later were rewarded with the laugh famous throughout the Bay Area. A magisterial boom that demanded notice, halted conversations, encouraged participation. Seeing Paul's tray, Gordy boomed again, then solemnly intoned, "Your humor hasn't evolved beyond Neanderthal, you mesomorphic gnome." He eased into the standard-sized cafeteria chair, blubbery backside more overhanging than on. Turning to Arlene, "You look magnificent, my dear. You should have gone blonde years ago." Arlene beamed. Paul said, "You do look great." He felt like an idiot.

Gordy asked, "Are you both free tonight?"

Paul said, "Yeah, quiet night planned," while Arlene shook her head

"Arlene, we'll go next week. Paul, cancel quiet." He snatched Paul's cell phone and dialed by heart. "Hello, reservations for two please. 6:30. C-O-M-B-E-S." Turning to Paul, "Pick me up at 6:00 and I'll tell you where. Your treat, as payment for the pain and suffering you just inflicted." Looking disdainfully at the bulging tray, "I guarantee you, my appetite won't be so skimpy."

Now anticipating a gourmet dinner, Paul skimped on lunch. Paul packed the barely shorn pyramid into a take-out box and carried it outside.

Gordy wriggled out of the front seat of Paul's '18 Prius and smoothed his jacket lapels. Extracting a dark blue tie from a pocket, he said, "Help me knot this. I never do it right." Paul said, "Uh oh, I didn't bring a tie."

"My fault, I forgot to tell you that ties are mandatory." Gordy's shoulders slumped. "I'll tell the hostess we have to cancel. What a shame, the food here is superb."

Paul ran his fingers through his dark black hair. "Gordy, I feel terrible. I should have checked. If you want to pick another restaurant for tonight, we can come back here next week."

He unlocked the passenger door. Gordy made no move to get in, suddenly snapped his fingers as a mischievous grin spread across his face. "We're in luck, I just remembered that I have an extra." He let Paul watch transfixed as slowly, gleefully, mimicking a stage magician, he pulled the tie through his fingers. It was a monstrosity. Glowing bright red with pictures of naked women cavorting on a beach, the tie had required a three-store search that afternoon. Paul held it at arm's length as if he'd been handed a dead skunk. Gordy took two steps back and nodded with vigorous admiration. "Magnificent! That tie epitomizes you." He grabbed Paul's elbow and dragged him into the lobby. To Paul's great relief, the maître d' intercepted them and suggested that he might feel more at ease with one of the ties kept handy for such emergencies.

Paintings by local artists hung from every wall of the newly refurbished Fourth Street restaurant. Pointing to a street scene of downtown Oakland, Gordy said, "I'm sure you didn't notice, but there's a similar one by the same artist hanging over my fireplace." He eased himself into the oversized chair, which accommodated him comfortably. "Tonight I elevate your taste to something more sophisticated than hotdogs and beans over a campfire."

A cup of leek soup was listed at ten dollars, most of the entrees in the mid-thirties. Gordy said, "Think I'll start with the chowder, then a Caesar salad. Their lobster is fantastic—flown in daily from Newfoundland." He beckoned to a hovering waiter. "Let's have a bottle of your best chardonnay." Paul, two weeks away from payday, wondered if he could get away with ordering a small salad (eight dollars and fifty cents).

"You're really expecting to pick up the bill, aren't you?"

"I'm willing to sacrifice a month's pay so my undernourished buddy doesn't starve to death. Besides, I need this time to change your mind about the ballgame."

Gordy shook his enormous head. "Forget it. The good news is that dinner's on me. I convinced Arlene to let me do a weekly restaurant review, so the station picks up the tab for GJ and guest. Naturally, I'll sample everything you order."

Paul wiped his brow with relief. "Gordy, you've got to play."

"Look, what do you weigh? One hundred eighty, one hundred eighty-five? Well, maybe you haven't noticed, but it's not just in intellect and charm that I have you doubled. Running is painful and embarrassing."

"Nobody expects you to get five hits. You're overweight, you smoke, and you eat like a bull elephant, but you're a hero to most of the Bay Area. Maybe if other fat degenerates saw you, they'd start exercising and getting healthy."

"You're such a sweet talker, I'm almost tempted. But KDFA always wins, so they get to donate the proceeds. I won't help support their Tory values."

"Losers donate twenty-five percent, and you can pick the charity. With you as an attraction, we'll get a great turn-out."

"Damn you, you're spoiling my appetite. Let's talk about less depressing stuff, like bulimia or genital herpes."

"Say yes."

"You ungrateful shit, this is my thanks for giving you the best meal of your boring little life. You think the fans want to see their favorite celebrity die of a heart attack? Alright, alright, but you have to break the news of my fatal coronary to my parents. Also, I'll give you the names of all my ex-girlfriends; I'll want a gigantic on-field suttee."

Brent Introduces Himself to Colfax

"... going twice, gone. Sold to number 142." Brent Willerman punched the air with his thick fists and shouted "Whooee, let the games begin!" Having bid far over value for a baseball signed by all the still-living 1969 Miracle Mets, he'd completed his collection. Brent owned a copy of *Huckleberry Finn* signed by Samuel Clemens, a rare Hummel figurine, an ivory inlaid wheelock pistol made in Saxony in the sixteenth century, and eight other items sure to captivate the intended recipients. That night his man Dominic wrapped each one and enclosed a short note.

Bronson Colfax had given his entire staff a rare day off. So, on his own, he heated a pot of water and searched for cold cereal. Squinting at the morning sun, he hobbled to the security gate for the newspaper. Sitting on top of the paper was a large envelope bearing his name. Colfax hitched up his shorts and stared with distaste. Probably a threatening note written by an ungrateful employee or eco-terrorist. The morons often tried to impress their equally moronic girlfriends by vandalizing his grounds. Previous notes had been accompanied by pictures of deformed frogs, dead birds, and scummed-up lakes. Colfax had mounted them for display at board meetings. Bending slowly on creaky knees, he picked up the envelope. It contained something rigid, though almost certainly too insubstantial to be dangerous. In the kitchen, he carelessly slit one side and watched a note on parchment flutter to the floor. He read, "After you authenticate my gift, show your appreciation by meeting me at the San Francisco Hyatt this week. Call

415-865-9626 for the room number and to set up a time. First class tickets will be sent. Sorry, no explanations till then. Brent."

The name Brent evoked no memories, and the motivation behind a gift was baffling, but the note's tone seemed innocuous enough. Back to the envelope, he ripped at two protective layers of cardboard. They fell away and, like an oyster opening its shell, revealed an extraordinary treasure. He grasped the table top for support. Miniature paintings were Colfax's passion, and this gem, a circle of gnomes dancing in an ocher woodland, was exquisite. A magnifying lens uncovered subtle details that reminded him of the works of Robert Hughes. He tilted the painting, held it to the light, moved around the magnifying glass, and became convinced that he did indeed hold a genuine Hughes.

Brent's TV monitor followed Colfax as he entered the lobby and handed twenty dollars to a desk clerk. "If I don't call within thirty minutes and say 'I need a laptop in Room 704,' send up security immediately." Colfax took no unnecessary risks. Brent listened to the reedy voice and thought of the one-time Presidential candidate H. Ross Perot. He snickered.

"Hey buddy, glad you could make it. C'mon in."

He gestured for Colfax to step inside the luxury suite and smiled reassuringly when the visitor remained in the doorway.

"Don't be so uptight. I'm about to make you a charter member of a very exclusive sporting fraternity."

Colfax advanced two small steps. "I intend to keep the Hughes, so I'll give you the courtesy of listening." He stood unmoving, waiting, in stark contrast to the bigger man's joviality.

"Of course you can keep the Hughes. Let's talk awhile, get to know each other." Colfax offered his hand hesitantly and immediately regretted it. Brent's powerful handshake sent a shockwave all the way to the smaller man's elbow.

"I didn't bring my trophy case, but here's some pictures. Check them out."

The first photograph in the large scrapbook featured a young man on a football field hoisting a trophy over his head. Brent expanded his chest. "That's me, Cotton Bowl, 1942, first lineman ever to win the MVP trophy. One sports reporter wrote that I was the meanest man in football."

"Football bores me."

He turned the page. Brent in a boxing ring, staring down at a flattened opponent. Colfax yawned.

"Hold on, I've got to make a call."

Brent's massive arm draped around Colfax's shoulder, effectively constraining him to the chair. "Won't take but a second." He dialed and said, loudly and distinctly, "I need a laptop in Room 704." Colfax's pale face turned even whiter. Brent released his grip. "Surprised, huh! Any hotel I stay at, the key staff are in my pocket. But don't worry, nothin' bad's gonna happen to you. Feel free to go whenever you want."

Annoyed with himself for having so stupidly walked into a potentially dangerous situation, Colfax struggled to appear calm. He carefully slowed his breathing and deepened his voice. "I will go unless you immediately tell me what this is about."

"As I said, I'm starting an exclusive fraternity. You're my first choice, because of your reputation as a daring and ruthless businessman. Also, because your sorrow inspired me to create a game that's more kick-ass than football. Others will be joining by the end of next week."

"My sorrow?"

Brent's teeth wrenched the cap off a beer bottle. "Here's the deal. Football was my best sport, but I was multi-talented. Four-letter man. Nowadays, after six knee surgeries and a hip replacement, even golf is a struggle. I hate just watching—last time I went to a baseball game I nodded out before the third inning. Besides, I resent that reserve infielders make almost as much money as people like us. I worked long hours for many years to build up my business. I know you did too."

Colfax didn't volunteer that he'd inherited his money. He

simply nodded and let the diatribe continue.

"My stomach's a wreck. What's the good of knowing almost every 4-star restaurant maitre'd in the country when I chew more Tums than lobsters. Sex? Once a month and lately as boring as baseball. Hearing about genocides and serial killers used to turn me on, but they're never done creatively any more. Papa Doc and Ted Bundy are dead."

Colfax understood the feeling. "It's nice when someone who hasn't seen me for awhile says 'You haven't changed a bit.' But you didn't fly me out here to complain about aging. What did you mean by 'my sorrow'?"

"Let's watch a video."

Brent inserted a tape into the VCR. "I first heard about you when that environmental geek showed up with a bullhorn outside your house a few years ago. The news stories made it seem like you were pretty pissed off."

Colfax winced. "That kike bastard. Edelman. Irving Edelman."

"Remember what happened afterward?"

"Some lefty judge fined him $100 and made him promise to be good. I wanted to kill them both."

Brent said, "My father had a bypass operation scheduled for that week. When he read the morning paper, he became so incensed his heart literally tore. After the funeral I vowed to make Edelman pay." Brent pressed the play button. "You're gonna love this."

The opening scene showed Edelman jogging with a small dog around Oakland's Lake Merritt. Colfax recognized his adversary immediately. The camera cut to a park in the Oakland hills. A young man wearing heavy protective clothes and thick gloves gave a thumbs-up sign, then donned a facemask. Poison oak thrives in the hills, growing profusely alongside walking trails and drooping pretty bright orange and green foliage from thick vines that occasionally exceed ten feet in height. The man collected two large plants and stuffed them in a trash bag. The next scene showed him in a kitchen, chopping the plants into small pieces and blending them with water until the mixture became a quart of green, murky liquid. He suctioned some into a squirt gun.

Back to Edelman jogging. The same young man held a piece of meat in his hands and watched until the dog briefly ran ahead out of Edelman's sight. He waved the meat until the dog loped over, then aimed the squirt gun. The next scene showed him holding up a sign reading "EDELMAN'S CAR." He squirted each door handle.

Colfax clapped. "Wonderful, seeing that pleases me as much as the Hughes. But I still don't—."

Brent swigged the beer. "There's more."

The man left a poison oak-impregnated newspaper outside the door to Edelman's small house, mailed him a letter dipped in poison oak, and while Edelman sat on the throne in the bathroom of a restaurant, replaced the soap with special bars. He rubbed the inside of a condom with the liquid and gave it to an elegant hooker. She contrived to have Edelman pick her up.

"Man, he must've had one helluvan itch. Will I get to see him scratching?"

Brent patted his belly. "Even better. My staff includes some highly skilled technicians."

In darkness outside Edelman's house, a man carrying several tools exited waving for the camera. Brent narrated. "He just tapped into Edelman's TV. We used a telephoto lens for the next part."

Edelman, relaxing on a comfortable chair in front of his TV, watched the Giants' battle the Braves—until a sixth inning Giants rally was interrupted by a pretend-roving TV reporter reading a "late-breaking news bulletin." The reporter described a mysterious disease responsible for twenty-seven deaths nationwide over a six-month period. Medical authorities had suppressed reports for fear of causing widespread panic, but the station believed in the public's right to know. In each documented case, victims had initially complained of a terrible rash accompanied by itching and general discomfort. Doctors had diagnosed poison oak, but most of the victims didn't remember being near the plant. The rash and itching typically disappeared after about a week, but then liver and kidneys began failing. The victims deteriorated rapidly and died excruciatingly painful deaths. All had been Jewish men of Eastern European heritage. In their thirties and of medium build. Like Edelman. The reporter gave the name of a physician/medical researcher on the trail of a cure, and she interviewed two specialists who called him the best in the business.

The next morning's specially doctored copy of the *Oakland Tribune* included a follow-up story. Edelman found it hard to read, being exhausted from having spent most of the previous night scratching. The article gave the doctor's phone number and urged everybody with matching symptoms and characteristics to call.

The receptionist urged Edelman to schedule an immediate appointment. She ushered him into a small waiting room set up for surreptitious videotaping, whereupon actor/Doctor Aristotle Venn ordered a series of expensive and painful laboratory tests. The following week, Venn confirmed Edelman's worst fear: he had contracted the dreaded disease. The compassionate "doctor" encouraged Edelman to have faith and prescribed expensive nutritional supplements, an exercise regimen of calisthenics at dawn, and a diet of boiled potatoes, okra, sardines, cod liver oil, and beet juice. Edelman had to abstain from sex and remain indoors when the outside temperature registered between forty and seventy-five degrees. (Oakland temperatures fall within that range more than ninety percent of the time.) He could not drive or even ride in a car. The symptoms would clear up within a couple of weeks but would recur unless he followed the regimen for an entire year. Edelman accepted every detail, as evidenced by scenes documented on video throughout 2019 and 2020. He obeyed Venn's periodic requests for additional tests and bloodletting.

Brent clicked off the VCR. Colfax said, "That's two I owe you."

"You just saw the solitaire version of a game I invented which became the most exciting thing in my life. Trouble is, I got bored playing on my own. Competition is my lifeblood, and I wanted worthy foes. So I decided to form a league. Too bad we'll have to play in secret, or else I'd be ranked someday with Abner Doubleday and James Naismith."

Marice

Joanna Soriano removed her shoes and tiptoed inside the small apartment to avoid waking her older sister. Seeing a light, she knocked and pushed open the bedroom door. Marice glanced up from her desk and smiled wearily, eyes drooping and whole body hunched over.

"What gives, Eece, it's not Halloween yet?" Then, gently, "You look terrible."

Marice held up the charcoal caricature for Joanna.

"Do you think Ygnacio will hate this? He came out kinda fat."

"He'll love it as long as it's got your signature on the bottom."

Marice shrugged and pulled out a fresh sheet of paper. "I'd better try again."

Joanna said, "It's after 11:00 and tomorrow's a big day. You don't want them to remember you as a sleepy old hag."

"Thanks for the encouragement. The other charcoals came out decently. I don't want Ygnacio to feel funny about his."

"You're a terrible role model for an impressionable kid sister. I'll probably end up as driven and neurotic as you."

Marice hated to withhold anything from her two-years younger sister, but this latest assignment had caused serious misgivings. Laughing, she said, "You stopped paying attention to me when you turned ten."

"Thanks for letting me stay here while you're in London. I won't break anything."

The dozen eighteen to twenty-four-year-olds from all over the country, the oldest only slightly younger than Marice, spent the morning hugging, exchanging gifts and addresses, and making fun of each other's caricatures. Toward noon she called them together.

"I just want to thank you guys. Being your team leader has been the best experience of my life."

Under her guidance, they had been encouraged to develop their own styles while teaching children how to read in one of the most disadvantaged schools in the state.

"I'll bet reading scores skyrocket next year at Castlemont," she said.

A young woman asked, "How long will you be away?"

"Only a week, but you'll all have moved on by then." She took one last photograph and walked toward the car. Looking back over her shoulder, "Now remember, all you little snots promised to write me when you get back home."

The Week of Apparent Miracles

By June 30, Paul had fulfilled every promise to himself. Two mile runs and 225 push-ups per day, plus gaining ten solid pounds. In the best shape of his life, he looked forward to teaching the jerks at KSMO a lesson.

Sunday, July 4, 2020 began the string of apparent miracles.

Apparent Miracle One: By the time the last player straggled onto the field, Paul realized that his optimism had been misplaced. KSMO's job announcements must have read "Substantial minor league experience required." They had recruited three former pros to their team, whereas Paul captained a group of dedicated nonathletes, most less coordinated than a bikini and earmuffs. At 185 pounds, he weighed close to the men's average, but nobody else approached that vicinity. Gordy Jackson and a second 300-pounder with plantlike speed and agility offset four men who were skinny bordering on invisible. None of the women players inspired hope that KDJM could avoid losing yet again.

Both stations had bombarded listeners with promotions. The baseball field in Golden Gate Park, adjacent to a picnic area and surrounded by redwood trees, is idyllic in July. So crowds numbered in the high hundreds and included reporters from the *San Francisco Chronicle*, *Oakland Tribune*, *San Jose Mercury News*, and TV channel 2.

The bad guys scored four quick runs and could have had more. But they showboated at every opportunity, and sloppy base running turned two doubles into outs. They made uncharacteristic errors in the field. When Gordy came to bat with one run in and a woman on second, the pitcher waddled around the mound in his version of great parody. Then he motioned the outfielders to come in closer. The leftfielder took two tentative steps, but the pitcher kept waving until he stood right behind the shortstop. The rightfielder threw his glove on the infield grass and covered the second baseman's eyes with his hands.

Having spent the entire morning persuading his reluctant friend not to renege on the promise to play, Paul yelled for them to stop making asses of themselves. When they continued, he strode angrily towards the mound. Two teammates caught up and restrained him. Grabbing his arms, they reminded him that the game was for charity.

Gordy and the next batter walked. As Paul stepped to the plate, the shortstop and left fielder pulled out corncob pipes and turned their backs toward home. They began puffing as though auditioning for a softball version of the Harlem Globetrotters. Paul glared but was secretly pleased—Gordy would realize he hadn't been singled out for ridicule.

The first pitch floated waist high, not very fast. Paul smashed it to left and watched the ball roll untouched into a privet hedge. Gordy slogged his way around the bases and plopped down gasping at home, leaving just enough room for two teammates to step on the plate behind him. The spectators applauded, even more so when he demanded that someone bring him a donut or he wouldn't move. After the third out, he claimed to be too winded to return to the field.

KSMO's antics kept the score close. In his next at-bat Paul doubled in two runs. When he strode to the plate in the next inning with the bases loaded, several spectators called him by name. Sneering at the pitcher, he gestured for the outfielders to move in closer. They stayed deep and in attentive crouches. The pitcher twice shook off the catcher's signs, then inexplicably threw another not-very fast fastball. Paul whacked it over the leftfielder's head. Grand slam homerun.

In the sixth inning, their lead cut to one run, KSMO loaded the bases. The clean up hitter smashed a vicious low line drive toward leftfield that eluded shortstop Paul's outstretched glove. KDJM's third baseman, in perfect position, reacted with the instincts of the clerk/typist he was—and dove out of harm's way. But the ball hit a baserunner and the umpire declared the batter out. The KSMO program director screamed in protest from the second row while the umpire turned his back and bent over to dust off home plate. The program director rushed onto the field to continue the argument. Players from both teams ran toward the plate and converged to trade insults. Several young men abandoned their seats to align with players of their favorite station. A few punches were thrown. The umpire threatened to end the game. Paul stayed out of the fray, unobtrusively retrieving the ball and waiting for the restoration of order. When the umpire called for play to resume, Paul casually walked toward the runner leading off second and tagged him. The umpire waved his arm with a flourish. "Out!"

The KSMO players swarmed the field, surrounding and cursing the umpire. Gordy reached into the ice chest and tossed beers to the KDJM players. They toasted each other on the sidelines. Two rowdier ones, proud to have brought the game down to the level of farce, mooned their discombobulated rivals.

By the time order was again restored, the din had attracted nearly every picnicker and weekend skater in the vicinity. Spectators ringed the entire field. Paul's final at-bat came with the tying run inching off third, producing the rivalry's first dramatic moment in years. While the pitcher, catcher, and shortstop conferred against a backdrop of obscenities from Paul's teammates, he crouched menacingly in the batter's box and took several powerful practice swings. Then the catcher crouched away from the plate and stuck out his glove. They intended to walk him intentionally. The spectators booed and launched a barrage of empty beer cans and half-eaten fruit onto the field, necessitating yet another lengthy delay.

Paul trotted to first base feeling positively Ruthian, and with the happy thought that his postgame ratings would skyrocket. He took a small lead, broke for second on the first pitch, and slid in safely. The next batter dribbled a slow grounder to second, and the runner on third beat the throw home. The ball bounced away from the catcher. Paul, legs churning wildly, never stopped running. He slid home just ahead of the catcher's throw to the pitcher covering. Final score, 19-18, KDJM.

His teammates mobbed him with more speed than they'd ever shown on a baseball field. The crowd surged forward whistling and applauding while reporters converged for interviews and picture-taking. Paul Combes spoke with lips fixed two inches higher at the corners than in the middle.

Brent's Exclusive Club

Twenty men, mostly Americans but also two Saudis, two Japanese, a German, a Frenchman, and a Brit, plus a planeload of chefs, valets, and other factotums, gathered in a seaside village in Cyprus. The combined age of the twenty was about 1,600 years and their combined assets greater than those of most medium-sized countries. In democratic fashion and with Robert's Rules strictly enforced, they discussed, debated, and hammered out rules and regulations for their new game. At first, a few people had trouble with the concept. A banker from Chicago failed to see the skill involved in torturing a bunch of suckers. Brent Willerman explained that the idea was to compete with other intelligent and creative people to see who could advance their targets to a difficult endpoint. One competitor might have to get the target to run naked onto the field during a baseball game, another to get him to claim to a reporter that he was abducted by aliens, another to adopt a Portuguese baby. The one to maneuver the target to the endpoint first would be the winner. Tormenting them was just a lagniappe.

Brent gave an example to help them decide on the propriety of felonies. "If you get your target to perform the required act by holding a gun to his head, you are committing an unesthetic, uncreative felony and will receive a low score. But if you convince your target that he is the reincarnation of Ghengis Khan, and he kills ten people, you'd make our highlight reels."

The German said, "But if one of us is caught committing a felony, couldn't we all be indicted as co-conspirators?"

"Ah, excellent question. I consulted my legal staff and am sure you'll all do the same. Here's their assessment. You'd be technically guilty, but most of you have committed felonies on a regular basis in the process of accumulating your wealth. You're too smart to be caught. You have no obvious motive and will be delegating authority, so you'll be far removed from the direct commission of felonious behaviors. In the extraordinarily unlikely event that one of you is caught, I hope you'd have enough decency not to implicate the rest of us."

Brent's game would let them compete at directing special live performances with the whole world as their set. Everybody was a potential cast member, and the targets would never know. (A small bloc failed to persuade the majority that the challenges would be more stimulating if targets were informed of their status.)

The Frenchman rose on wobbly legs. "The great French philosopher Descartes imagined a powerful evil genius who exerted all his energies toward deceiving humanity. Brent, you are an evil genius. I salute you for letting me participate."

"I don't know shit about philosophy, but if this game qualifies me as a genius, I love it all the more."

The Frenchman stood again: "One more point. Descartes' demon fooled all humanity. To emulate him, we should try for quantity as well as quality. The more targets the better."

Brent raised both hands. "Whoa, take your time. We can modify the rules as we gain experience."

The older of the two Japanese men said, "Names are important. We must bestow one that captures the deep implications of our sporting venture." Several men applauded. After much discussion, they agreed on "Ontological (describing the philosophy of ultimate reality) Configurations."

A calligrapher brought in for the occasion inscribed the consensually-arrived at rules in gold lettering on vellum. He made twenty copies. What follows is the original version.

ONTOLOGICAL CONFIGURATIONS

Ontology is the philosophy of ultimate reality. In the game of ontological configurations, each player (P) strives to manipulate the reality and thus the overt behavior of a preselected target (T). The game has three variants.

INDEPENDENT TARGETS: Each P is given a separate T to lead through a series of predesignated behaviors. The objective is to get T to the behavioral endpoints with creativity and flair.

SINGLE TARGET: A single T is selected and each P is given a different endpoint. The game ends whenever T reaches one of the endpoints.

SINGLE TARGET, LIFETIME PERFORMANCE: A single T is selected for each P. P has free reign in manipulating T's reality.

Points will be awarded based on esthetic factors and economy of effort. Although Ps will be free to choose their methods, physical violence will generally be considered unesthetic. Even threatening violence or committing any other felony, unless done with exceptional flair and creativity, will result in deduction of points.

Ps may interfere with the efforts of other Ps, subject to restrictions imposed by the rules committee. A panel of 3 judges will assign points to each P for each event, on a scale ranging from 0 to 10. Judges have the discretion to give special prizes for exemplary performances.

Lifetime performances will be rewarded as appropriate.

New games begin on the first Monday of each month, and play shall be rotated between the 2 brief forms. Each P will be permitted to have a staff of up to 50, including writers, actors, researchers, and technicians.

The rules committee shall propose changes as they see fit. Each proposed change shall be put into effect only with the approval of at least 2/3 of the Ps. The rules committee shall also set the salary for judges. The selection committee shall interview prospective judges as vacancies arise. Candidates must receive the approval of at least 2/3 of the Ps. Judges serve for life unless 3/4 of the members vote for impeachment. The selection committee shall also choose Ts. No formal criteria exist for selection. The assessment committee shall determine players' fees. (The current one-time membership fee is 1 million dollars, and the annual fee is $50,000.) At the end of each year, all excess money shall be turned over to the research committee. The committee shall maintain a library and a laboratory available to all Ps. Results of research conducted with money from the common fund must be shared with all Ps, but Ps may conduct independent researches, in which case they are not obligated to share results. The secrecy committee is entrusted with the task of ensuring that word of the game does not reach the general public. No restrictions are placed on its methods. If necessary, the secrecy committee shall call an emergency session of the executive council.

Each committee shall consist of 3 members elected for staggered 3-year terms. Elections will be held annually for one new member for each committee each year. No P with the exception of Brent Willerman may serve on more than one committee at a time. The executive council shall comprise 5 members elected for a 3-year term. Brent Willerman shall serve on the executive council in perpetuity.

Marice in London

"... *IN ERMINES AND PEARLS. That's why the Lady is a tra...*" Marice reached for the snooze button on her travel radio/alarm to shut Ella down. Ten minutes later, she dragged herself out of bed while Sinatra did things his way. Morning one in London and she'd awakened to American classics. While rubbing a wet washcloth across her eyes, she smelled strong coffee in the hallway. Still in her nightie, she opened the door and peeked out. In front stood a small cart with a freshly brewed pot, a container of orange juice, and the *Guardian*. She called room service and ordered eggs and toast. Expecting the next few days to be the worst of her life, she intended to start on a full stomach.

The dull gray morning deepened Marice's dark mood. She trudged off aimlessly, without an umbrella and in a light sweater that gave little protection against a steady, cold drizzle. Arms curled against her chest, she reached the corner just as a double-decker bus pulled up in front of the hotel and discharged a group of mostly young, animated couples. Its arrival offered a welcome diversion. She ran back, hopped on, and settled in for London sightseeing with commentary from a knowledgeable guide. As they approached the Tower of London, she listened to his account of the two princes who had been imprisoned by their wicked uncle. At Trafalgar Square, she learned that the model for the sculpted lion had actually been a large dog.

She got off at the National Gallery. In a college art class five years earlier, she had painted a boating scene with heavy emphasis on oranges and blues. Her instructor had circled the easel with head cocked and face devoid of expression. While the rest of the class worked silently on their own projects, Marice awaited his verdict as though she were a murder defendant. As he started to speak, a drop of blood fell from her left pinkie, pierced by the nail on her right hand. When he said that the painting reminded him of Renoir's *Boating on the Seine*, she hugged him, then stepped back and giggled with embarrassment. He grinned while the other students whistled and shouted encouragement. After class, Marice bought a print of the Renoir and had since often dreamed of viewing the original at arm's length.

Even more glorious than she'd imagined, the Renoir made her realize that the instructor had commented to inspire rather than as an art critic. Still, under other circumstances she would have been overjoyed by the experience. Instead, she left shortly afterwards for needed shopping.

Another of the ubiquitous tour buses waited outside. On her next pass around the Square, a new guide, as self-assured as the first, explained that the model for the lion sculpture had been a stuffed lion. Well, she wasn't there for educational purposes. She disembarked in Kensington and walked to Harrod's.

She and two wide-eyed teenage friends, feeling incredibly sophisticated and sybaritic, had once spent a day exploring San Francisco's Neiman-Marcus. Now, sipping #14 tea in Harrods' Food Court, she concluded that Neiman-Marcus had been merely decadent. In this regal establishment, she wouldn't have blinked at seeing the queen trying on tiaras. She visited the cosmetic and women's clothing departments and left carrying several of Harrods' chic green bags.

Back at the hotel, Marice scowled at her reflection. Make-up plastered on so she'd pass for white, dress too tight, cleavage bursting out. She imagined her parents inspecting her and shuddered. She'd explained that her role as escort was to attend interesting functions with respectable but unattached men who paid well for the accompaniment of a stunning companion. No funny business involved. As it turned out, several of her dates had tried to start up a romance, but payment was not contingent on her decision. Most had been charming, accomplished, and influential, and two had become friends. Her parents had listened, but in the end they still equated "escort" with "prostitute."

After she'd been on the job six months, her employer asked her to take on a special assignment.

"You know who Grady McCallum is, right?"

She nodded at the rhetorical question. McCallum's notoriety extended throughout the Bay Area. He dominated the city council in Danville, a picturesque town about fifteen miles east of Oakland. Situated in liberal northern California, Danville was a bastion of white conservatism and McCallum its spokesman. If he'd been honest, he'd have campaigned on the Hate Platform. He opposed affirmative action, wanted much tighter immigration laws, believed that AIDS was God's way of punishing homosexuals for their bestiality, and opposed disarmament, the environmental movement, and most of the American Constitution (except the right of citizens to bear Uzis). An effective, highly quotable speaker, his words often made headlines in the Oakland and San Francisco papers. During his seven years in office, racial tensions in Danville had increased considerably. In one noteworthy sequence of events, he gave an impassioned speech on the evils of the welfare system to a wildly appreciative audience. Two days later a gang of twelve-year-old white kids, shouting "McCallum for President," beat up and severely injured an elderly Vietnamese man.

"You couldn't pay me enough to be in the same room with him."

Her employer smiled. "Have you heard of Jack Callahan?"

She hadn't. "He's a politician in London. If McCallum has a soul mate—."

"McCallum has no soul."

"If McCallum has a soul mate, it's Callahan. You can help destroy his career."

Her employer explained the details. Marice said no. He said, "The pay is veeery good. Twenty-five thousand dollars for a few days' work. You'll be able to buy yourself a car." She shook her head. He said, "Let me show you some recent articles about him."

Staring at the floor-length mirror, Marice wondered if her parents had been right. All she saw was a cheap hooker. Fingering the dress's still-attached price tag, she corrected herself. Not cheap at all. Very expensive call girl. Still, though she dreaded the next few days, she'd have taken the assignment for free.

The tall Pakistani stood propped against his cab. Dressed in filthy, tattered jeans and a tee-shirt portraying two dogs having sex, he didn't fit Marice's stereotype of the proper British working class. He stubbed out a cigarette and motioned her to get in. He didn't leer, for which Marice felt grateful. She said, "Please take me to Hyde Park."

"American, yes!" She nodded, and he said, "Last month would have been better. The daffodils and crocuses were blooming."

"Thank you. I'm going to Speaker's Corner."

He swiveled round from the driver's seat. "Jack Callahan will be there tonight."

"Yes, I know."

"You're not one of them, are you?"

She nodded.

He stared for several seconds, then waggled his finger at her and the door. "Out. My cab does not service fascists."

She told the next driver that she wanted to walk around the garden.

Marice arrived well before the 6:00 starting time to secure a spot in front. By 6:00 about 1,000 people, mostly manual laborers who had come directly from work, packed the area and suffused the air with pungent, sweaty odors. Four demonstrators waved signs denouncing Callahan. They stood on the periphery, close to the bobbies.

At 6:05, Callahan swaggered on stage dressed in shorts and an XX large shirt with sleeves slit to expose his massive arms. He dropped to his knees and assumed a weightlifter's pose. The crowd screamed his name, whistled, and stamped their feet. An attractive woman sashayed onto the platform. Callahan removed her raincoat, revealing a Union Jack shirt underneath. Hoisting her effortlessly above his head, he shouted, "Isn't she lovely! Isn't the UK flag lovely! Let's hear it for the UK!" The roar of approval hurt Marice's ears. She added to it.

"But the Pakis think this country is theirs. Here's the Paki flag." A thin man pranced across the stage. Made up to look grotesquely ugly, he had a Pakistani flag sewn onto his rear end. Callahan ripped off the patch to expose the man's buttocks. "This is what I think of their flag." He stepped on it, spit, picked his nose and threw it on the torn fabric. "This is what I think of Pakis." His confederate ran off cowering in mock terror.

That was only the opening act. Callahan reviled Turks, Senegalese, and eventually virtually everybody except white Protestant British working class soccer fans. He accused the others of undermining the morality of the entire nation and urged them to return to their backward homelands. Although Marice's anxiety level skyrocketed, the audience's enthusiasm eliminated any lingering moral uncertainties.

When the rally ended, Callahan hawked autographed copies of *Wail for Brittania.* Marice waited in a long line. When her turn came, she scribbled her phone and room numbers on a piece of paper and clipped it to a ten-pound note. She said, "I'd love to hear more about your ideas."

Callahan exaggerated her American accent in falsetto. "Did you come all the way from Iowa just for this?"

"You have many fans in the states. When I was picking a vacation spot, the chance to hear you swayed me to London."

"Bollocks. Why are you here?"

"To persuade you to go on a speaking tour of the U.S."

Callahan fingered the ten-pound note, looked at the address she'd written, and rolled his tongue across his upper lip. "Lucky for you, my wife is out of town. I'll be done here in an hour."

She had drawn the line at getting nude or joining him in bed but had agreed to the rest. Make sure the room door is unlocked. Pour drinks. Ask him to get comfortable. Close the bathroom door, wash off make-up, accentuate Hispanic features, and strip to bra and panties. Go slowly to give him time to take off his clothes. Cough loudly as you reenter the bedroom. Her employer's henchmen would burst in. With one man holding a gun to keep him passive, the other would take lots of pictures. They'd be distributed to every tabloid in the city, but (she was assured) not across the ocean. She'd fly home and Callahan, career ruined for having an extramarital relationship with a brown-skinned woman, would never be able to track her down. She'd buy lots of goodies for everyone in the family and a new computer for La Raza. Then she'd return to her job as counselor there.

Now, trapped in a windowless cell, confronted with the enormity of her commitment, she heard cabinets being opened and slammed shut on the other side of the bathroom door. She reasoned, correctly, that Callahan was checking her personal effects. Marice gripped the washbasin to steady her shaking legs. Had she left any receipts in a jacket pocket, anything in the luggage that would reveal her identity? She heard the mini-bar open. Good, he hadn't found anything and was taking a drink. Then, unmistakable sound of a zipper being undone, clothes landing on a chair.

Marice silently cursed her reflection. "Dad was right. You're a sleazebag." She washed and washed and wasn't sure she could leave the bathroom. The door rattled. She jumped back and watched it vibrate. Callahan yelled, "I didn't come to get in tune with my own body. Get your ass out here."

She hadn't been given a contingency plan in case the men arrived late. Callahan shouted, "Open the fucking door or I'm coming in." With the water running full blast, she barely made out the words but had no doubt about their meaning. She thought she heard a second voice, then a crash as though something big had fallen. She whimpered, "I'll be out right away." No response. She waited, counted to ten, counted to 100. With no other viable options, she said "I'm coming out now" and opened the door.

Callahan lay motionless, blood flowing from a bullet hole in his temple, dead or imminently so. Before she could scream a tall black man stepped from behind the closet, wagged a finger attached to a silencer, and whispered "Shh."

He looked back. "John, check her out. This Chiquita is hot." A white man emerged, holding a camera. "Wow," he agreed. "Looks like Jennifer Lopez, only sexier. Hey Jenny, smile for the camera." Then, menacingly, "I think she wants me."

An open bottle of champagne sat on a small nightstand beside the dead man's head. The gunman said, "John, break out the cups." To Marice, "Pour."

John extended the cups toward Marice. She stood statue-like except for trembling.

Samuel said, "Don't worry, John's harmless. I'm the psychotic killer. Now fill those cups. No sense wasting good champagne." They must have seen the film *Pulp Fiction* and were trying to emulate actors Samuel Jackson and John Travolta.

She'd left her dress on a chair. With eyes fixed on the two men, she wriggled in while they watched. John grabbed his crotch and Samuel rolled his eyes, but they didn't interfere. John extended the cups again and ordered her to pour. A considerable quantity ended on the floor. Samuel smiled. "Don't worry, your future isn't in waitressing and the rug's already ruined. Pour yourself some, but aim for the cups this time."

She shook her head. He said, "It's criminal to drink good liquor out of paper cups, but we don't want to leave fingerprints. Oh yeah," he laughed, "I forgot. You just put your pretty fingers on the bottle. Besides, we are criminals." John retrieved the bottle with a gloved hand. "Your dearly departed had bad manners. He drank champagne while you were in the bathroom. Now the bottle has two sets of fingerprints."

Whimpering, "What are you going to do?"

Samuel put his hand into his back pocket. Marice flinched, but he was only extracting an envelope. "Just pay you. Here's your money plus a bonus for being so gorgeous. It's enough to buy a nice hacienda. There's also a plane ticket for the 7:30 A.M. flight to New York from Heathrow and from NY to San Francisco. The itinerary is written down. You've got reservations at the Connaught Hotel for tonight. It's even swankier than this one. Now walk calmly out of here. We'll clean up."

Marice took the envelope. Holding arms protectively in front of her chest, she edged past them maintaining the greatest distance possible. He added, "Of course, if you'd rather stay and entertain John and me, we could make the time."

Leonard

Leonard Watkins snarled the words, "Vengeance is mine, white boy, vengeance is mine." He straightened his shoulders and repeated the mantra, changing the inflection slightly to see which rendition sounded more menacing. Clutching two envelopes, heart racing with anticipation, he quickened his pace. Two teenage girls in skimpy shorts and tops skipped past him. They smiled, possibly to show off their newly implanted tongue rings. Their curvy bodies, unprotected from the morning sun, had already changed color from pink grapefruit to ripe tomato. Leonard smiled back, bemused by the compulsion of so many of them to expose themselves to UV radiation—one more datum proving that most whites were morons. A good ad campaign could probably persuade them that getting AIDs was chic.

Leonard expected his quarry to be sitting in his study absorbed at a computer, back facing the door. He planned to crawl in through a window generally kept wide open on hot summer days, but crawling proved unnecessary—the front door stood slightly ajar. Leonard gently pushed until the opening was wide enough for his head and he could peek into the room. The fool sat on an easy chair wearing headphones, relaxed posture suggesting closed eyes. Leonard unlaced his squeaky new sneakers and tiptoed up to the chair. A cat jumped off the man's lap and skittered to another room. He stirred momentarily, then resumed a slow and rhythmic breathing.

Post-Softball

The team celebrated the softball victory at a bar in Oakland, on San Pablo Avenue. The bartender refused to let Paul pay for food or drink. Several beers and a few hours later, he lay in bed dreaming that Clayton Kershaw refused to pitch to him, saying he belonged in a higher league.

Apparent Miracle Two: Paul usually slept late on Mondays in his small North Oakland house, but the doorbell woke him about 7:00. Stumbling down the stairs groggy but still in Heroland, he reached the door in time to see two friends drive off. They'd delivered a bouquet of roses and chrysanthemums. A platter of fresh fruit, smoked salmon, and bagels. The most recent issues of *Sports Illustrated*, *Playboy*, *Scientific American*, and *Writers Digest*. A calligraphed, framed version of the 3 x 5 index card that he'd hung next to pig-man. Henry Stapp's *Mind, Matter, and Quantum Mechanics*. And a big card with a cartoon muscleman on the front, signed by the entire station staff. They hadn't missed a trick.

Calling all the signatories took a good part of the morning. He put on a Jean Pierre Rampal CD, made a pitcher of lemonade, opened the *Sports Illustrated*, and sank into a huge leather chair that had cost fifty dollars at a garage sale. Although he enjoyed Rampal, music never stirred him, never filled him with passion. Paul envied friends who cried or broke into a sweat listening to a particularly moving piece. For him, music merely provided pleasant accompaniment to whatever else he was doing. Cranberry sauce, not turkey.

After his remarkable feats of the previous day, reading about the pennant races seemed plebeian. The music hypnotized, and the chair created a feeling of weightlessness. Eyes drooped and closed. Not quite asleep, not fully conscious, his head filled with glorious images.

Not for long! Leonard arrived and, with one swift motion, yanked off the headphones and jerked Paul's head upwards. "Vengeance is mine, white boy. Ven—." Paul sprang to alertness. Leonard, green eyes shining incongruously from dark brown face, began laughing uncontrollably. So much so that he couldn't shout out the second "vengeance." He finally caught his breath and said, "Hey farmboy, I tol' you to lock the door when you have that thing on. Else you gonna take it off someday and find your living room gone. This ain't Kansas, you know."

Paul's heart rate slowly decelerated. "Damn Leonard, you nearly decapitated me. There's coffee in the kitchen."

"Got no time. Gonna meet some friends at Stinson Beach. Wanna go?"

"I can't. Now what is this vengeance crap?"

"Remember when you scheduled me for the show and then booted me off at the last minute?"

"Sure, that was the day bin Laden was killed."

"Right, some trivial shit like that. Well, check this out." He handed Paul an envelope containing an invitation for Leonard to appear on the CBS *Morning Show*.

"Those people recognize talent. They called me one of the rising young novelists in America."

Paul jumped up and hugged his friend. "Fantastic! Congratulations Leonard, I'm so proud of you." Then, deadpan, "But aren't you embarrassed to play angry black man when you drive a Lexus, eat at Chez Panisse once a month, and spend mornings soaking your fat ass in your hot tub."

Leonard said as though as an afterthought, "Listen tight butt, I got something for you too." He flipped a second envelope toward Paul. "You ain't as hopeless as I thought."

Inside was a check for seventy-five dollars and a letter advising

Paul that his short story had won honorable mention in the *Northpoint* writing contest. He could now officially claim to be a writer. He whooped like a cowboy and hugged Leonard again.

Leonard pointed to the list of names on the letterhead. "You deserved it, it was a helluva good story, but don't tell anybody you slept with one of the judges."

"Hey, if that's what it took, I might have slept with you. But you wouldn't have been my first choice."

Leonard traced his finger along Paul's right cheek. "Looks like you're gonna have a permanent scar. Big deal, you were ugly to begin with."

Paul shoved him away. "I should have let those rednecks beat the crap out of you."

They reminisced about celebrating the acceptance of Leonard's first novel three years earlier, then Paul bragged about his baseball brilliance of the previous day. If Leonard's Stinson Beach friends had anticipated morning activities, they would have to revise their plans. Leonard finally said goodbye about an hour later. Paul's mom didn't answer the phone, so the mirror was his only companion. He winked, not sure if the handsome reflection reminded him more of Babe Ruth or Dosteovsky.

Giddy and eager to share the feeling, Paul called two close friends. One was busy and the other out. Unwilling to be mortal again just yet, he sauntered to Andronicos supermarket. A young couple waved and the man called out, "Hey, it's Paul Combes! We always listen to your show, and we saw the game yesterday. You were phenomenal." He waved back, distance from corners to middle of lip matching that of the previous day. He loaded a shopping cart with beer, licorice, ice cream, and other indulgences. Wheeling the cart down the produce aisle, he abruptly paused to juggle three oranges. To try to juggle. Just as the third soared upward, a young mother screamed at her boisterous son. Paul turned his head and mortality struck. The oranges bounced on the floor and rolled away along erratic paths. Too late, he yelled "Watch your step." An elderly man squished one and struggled to retain his balance while a woman kicked another all the way to the fresh berries section. Paul scurried to retrieve it.

Marice Meets Brent

Marice went to confession for the first time in three years but made no mention of the murder. She told of her single sexual encounter during the previous twelve months and assorted other accumulated sins. The list was strikingly trivial—she wouldn't have been shocked to hear snoring sounds from the other side of the confessional. Joanna, her sole confidante, advised against going to the police. Whatever the ultimate intentions of the murderers, they had planned well and held incriminating evidence. She tried contacting the escort agency but reached only a disconnected phone and vacant office. She located a newsstand on 14th Street selling British papers and stopped there each day for a week on her way to work. Both the *London Times* and *Daily Telegraph* headlined the Callahan murder. They quoted a high-ranking official that round-the-clock police activity had not turned up any leads. Nobody mentioned a mysterious woman. While politicians from each major party denounced the violence, Callahan followers vandalized an Asian neighborhood and sent several people to hospitals.

Marice made an appointment with a psychotherapist but cancelled an hour before the first scheduled session. Two weeks after her return to the U.S., her mail included a card written in gold lettering:

> YOU ARE CORDIALLY INVITED TO ATTEND A FASCINATING DISCUSSION CONCERNING A RECENT MURDER IN A LONDON HOTEL. REGRETS ONLY (MIGHT LEAD TO VERY SERIOUS REGRETS)

Marice leaned her bicycle against a flowering maple tree. No need for a lock—not in this fancy Piedmont neighborhood. A powerfully built man admitted her into a spacious living room and pointed to one of six luxurious sofas. "Sit," he commanded. Then he left. Alone, she stared straight ahead with shoulders rigid and reflected on her continued amazing stupidity. Maybe tomorrow, she thought bitterly, she'd wear a sandwich board saying "PLEASE RAPE OR MURDER ME." The ambience did nothing to reassure. Mounted on the far wall hung the head of a young polar bear. The trophy from a helicopter safari had a blood-stained arrow protruding from its lower jaw. Directly underneath stood a replica of Florida's Old Sparky electric chair.

The man returned a few minutes later to announce, "Your host." Brent Willerman swaggered in through a hallway, considerable bulk concealed inside a bright red caftan, cheerful countenance in marked contrast to hers. He said, "How ya doing Marice, I'm Brent." Winking, "Great work in London. Now let me tell you about your next job. I'm gonna make an offer you can't refuse."

"I'm not the right person. I've been crying every day."

Brent laughed, "Aw, sweetie, you're so delicate. Let me assure you, my men cleaned up the room and removed all traces of you. In fact, they moved Callahan's body to another hotel, so the boobies, oops, bobbies, will never come close to the truth."

"That's a relief, but I won't do anything like that again."

His voice turned icy. "Let me amend my last statement. The boobies would never come close to the truth without my help. But I don't have to keep the photographs and fingerprints locked in a safe place."

"What do you want?"

"That's better. Here's the deal." Brent whistled, "Dominic, bring our guest some tea and cookies." Then, crooking his finger, "Come see my fish." He offered his hand, but she waited for him to move away and take the lead.

Hugging a wall, taking tiny steps, spilling tea when he unexpectedly scratched his head, she followed him until he stopped at a small room next to the master bedroom. He pointed to a comfortable-looking chair. "Sit and watch the aquarium for awhile. Drink your tea. Something interesting will happen soon."

The well-stocked, enormous aquarium was home to dozens of brightly colored fish, snails, and plants. A water pump gurgled relaxing sounds. But, though a marked improvement over the bear head/electric chair, the tranquil scene didn't soothe Marice. While Brent hovered over her slurping beer, her muscles tightened—she did not anticipate enjoying the "interesting" surprise.

Two large, graceful angel fish undulated into view followed by a pair of dwarf gouramis and a zebra fish. A quartet of iridescent, multicolored beauties glided by. Despite her foreboding, Marice marveled. Suddenly, without warning, a two-inch needle shot up from the bottom of the tank, ricocheted off a glass pane, and crashed harmlessly back into the gravel. Her shoulders shook and tea spilled onto her shirt. The fish swam in frenzied circles for a few seconds, then resumed their leisurely movements.

"What just happened?"

"I saw a similar contraption in an art show several years ago. My fish lead a pleasant existence except that needles—in effect, miniature spears—discharge hourly from one of ten different places. If they make contact, they're lethal. I've had to replace so many fish, the pet store owner probably thinks I eat them."

Marice turned away. "You're barbaric."

"Nature is barbaric. This serves to remind me. Of course, being on guard doesn't always help." He yelled, "Dominic, bring me a chair."

Brent leaned back, arms folded against chest, and closed his eyes. Marice sat in her wet shirt, gaze averted from the aquarium.

"Three years ago Callahan ripped my father off for millions, though nothing could be proven in court. One month later the old man blew his brains out, and I swore I'd kill the bastard someday. Thanks, couldn't have done it without you. Your next assignment is strictly business. I'm being paid to fix a situation that's a cliché. Daughter of wealthy parents gets involved with lowlife. Long rap sheet, married twice, both wives died under suspicious circumstances. They're sure he's in it for the money." Brent waved expansively. "I fix things. Look around, you can see that my work pays well."

She pushed away the cookies. "I won't participate, no matter how reprehensible the person."

"Listen Mother Teresa, you sold your soul when you took that London trip, but it got you enough money to feed ten Mexicans for a year. I'm offering your soul back. Follow up your sparkling debut with another good job and we'll be quits."

She repeated, barely audibly, "What do you want?"

"Meet this guy. Go out a few times. Get him to fall in love with you. It should be easy, you are one hot babe. We'll be taking pictures and recording conversations."

"Are you going to hurt him?"

"Naw, no need. My payoff comes when he's done with the rich guy's daughter. You might even fall for him, which would make me no difference. Apparently, he does have a certain charm."

Brent told her to buy a car. "You've got money from the London job and you may have to move on short notice."

Marice Meets Paul

The dreaded phone call came a few days later. "Target has left home. I will follow and report his movements. Get ready to engage."

A second call came soon afterwards. "He's parking in the Andronicos supermarket lot on Telegraph Avenue."

Marice drove the short distance. (*This Paul must be pretty smooth. People at the game seemed to like him. Brent swore he wouldn't be hurt. But Brent's a cold-blooded killer. Oh Lord, please don't let anybody else die because of me. Please give me guidance.*) She parked and took a shopping cart. Brent had emphasized that the meeting appear adventitious.

Marice stood by her empty cart near the checkout counter, pretending to read a magazine while trying to work up the nerve to approach him. (*Okay witch, get it over with.*) She rolled the cart in his direction. When an orange came rolling toward her, she picked it up and forced a giggle.

The Biggest Apparent Miracle of All, Monday Afternoon: Paul spotted her. (*Wow, what a gorgeous woman! Stop ogling. The juggling stunt was bad enough, the way you're staring she'll expect to see drool.*) Too embarrassed to speak, he reluctantly turned the shopping cart toward the next aisle. Providence intervened in the person of the produce delivery man. Produce man had seen Paul's orange juggling stunt and recognized a macho, devil-may-care soul mate. Lacking Paul's inhibitions, he grinned from a vantage point behind Marice and thrust his pelvis vigorously—maybe to show how he'd handle the wench, maybe for male bonding.

(*What an idiot. Should I say anything and call even more attention to myself? I've got to. That creep would probably laugh if someone toilet papered the Mona Lisa.)* Paul strode past her and thrust out his chest. "That was rude. My fiancée deserves an apology."

Produce man mumbled an apology and skittered away. Marice was thankful—he'd made her job easier.

An elderly woman paused from sampling grapes and called for somebody to get the manager. Smiling at Marice, gesturing approvingly toward Paul, "You must be very proud. Respectful men are in short supply."

"He's never treated me with anything but full respect." Fighting back a feeling of revulsion, she winked and kissed him on the cheek. "Thanks, honey."

The woman went back to munching while Paul patted his cheek disbelievingly. He extended his hand. "If you're my new fiancée, you should know my name. I'm Paul."

"Hi, mine's Marice. I'm not sure what happened, but you apparently saved me from a terrible ordeal. Thanks." He bowed, adding Lancelot to his character mix.

She said, "If we're going to spend the rest of our lives together, I should know your last name too."

"Paul Andrew Combes. Professional subject. At your service."

Marice jumped up and clapped her hands with simulated joy. "I recognize you. I went roller skating in Golden Gate Park yesterday and stopped to watch the softball game. You're the heroic number 12."

"Were you there? I can't believe I missed you."

"You didn't miss much else."

"I finally took the uniform off just before coming here. Things were growing inside."

She flexed her biceps. "They call me BIG MAMA. Meanest wrestler this side of Laredo." She had never acted so silly with a man, but she wanted to dissociate herself as much as possible from the real Marice.

"I meant it about being a professional subject. I host a radio talk show and write fiction in my spare time. Till the radio job came up, I paid the bills by hiring out as a subject for psychology experiments, nutrition studies, drug studies, market surveys. I've had my spinal fluid tapped, I—"

She forced a giggle. "That's crazy. Does your writing pay?"

"Ha! For me, a big pay day is a year's free subscription to a small literary magazine. I've submitted dozens of Nobel Prize quality manuscripts, but Nobel must have misplaced my phone number."

"I'm entertaining tomorrow. Can you deliver two quarts of spinal fluid by three?"

Produce man returned to spray water on lettuces and other vegetables, keeping himself as far away as possible from the fruit section. Marice wondered if he worked for Brent. Or maybe the grape sampler did.

"Absolutely," said Paul. "And if it doesn't arrive on time, you pay nothing and I'll personally escort you to the restaurant of your choice. I'll need your name, address, and phone number."

She found a scrap of paper and wrote "Marice Soriano" and her phone number but not the address. Even so, she wondered if moving would be necessary once the ordeal was over. Paul smiled casually, feeling terribly dishonest, and folded the paper into his pocket. The honest response would have been to jump forty feet into the air shouting "Hallelujah."

At the dairy case, they encountered the lead singer with a well-known local band. Paul and Cody Certner had met at a station party and discovered a mutual addiction to handball. Equally matched, they'd become steady opponents. Cody poked Paul in the ribs and rolled his tongue at Marice.

"I was going to call you tonight. Heard you were sensational yesterday. Great job against those KSMO clowns." Paul beamed. "Listen, I've got two tickets to the Belafonte concert Friday at the Greek theater. I'd love to watch one legend with another sitting next to me. Interested?"

Paul patted Marice's cheek. He was gaining confidence. "Thanks Cody, I'm tied up this weekend. Besides, you're the only legend around here."

Cody shook his long hair and spoke to Paul while leering at Marice. "This may be Belafonte's last Bay Area performance. You earned the right to go. Come by the pad later and I'll give you the tickets."

Paul said, "Fantastic" and pulled out his wallet. Cody waved it off. "I can see I'm not your dream date at the moment." He struck the winsome pose that drove female fans wild and strutted off down the aisle.

She bought a few grocery items, and Paul helped load them into her car. He commented on their lightness. "You're not eating properly. Those other wrestlers will make mincemeat of you." She asked for advice and he recommended a restaurant known for its hearty portions. "But they have a strict rule against serving skinny female wrestlers unaccompanied by a talk show host. If you can't find anyone else, it would be my duty as a humanitarian to take you."

Alone in the car, Marice acknowledged to herself that the bastard had a certain amount of charm. He had seemed pleasant and witty, almost an anti-Callahan. She felt terrible for the daughter of Brent's client who, because of Marice's help, would soon be devastated.

The focus of Marice's animosity stood euphorically in the parking lot scribbling notes for a poem. He hadn't written poetry in years, but inspiration beckoned. He'd compare her skin to marble smoothed by millennia of rushing mountain waters. He'd call her a palette for an extraordinary blend of colors: sandalwood skin like eggs from healthy chickens; teeth like the first snow on Pikes Peak; eyes like springtime grass; waist-length hair as black as a starless night. He laughed aloud, realizing how strongly the similes betrayed his rural Kansas birthplace. A half-hour later, first draft almost done, he remembered his own groceries and ran back into the store. The shopping cart sat where he'd left it, ice cream dripping through the bottom. He confessed to a clerk and tipped him five dollars for mopping up the mess.

A Gaggle of Geezers

The elderly men squeezed into an ordinary-sized living room with only one service person to attend all of them. Unaccustomed to such austerity, they handled it grumpily. Dominic, always two steps behind, rushed around frantically taking orders for food and drinks. "Hey waiter, over here!" "Boy, I ordered a sandwich ten minutes ago!" "How long does it take to get a frigging Perrier!" Wine bottle in each hand, he allowed himself to imagine that each was an old fart's neck. He loosened his grip to avoid bloodying his hands on shattered glass.

When everybody seemed as comfortable as possible, Brent clapped and called for quiet. "I know from private conversations that you've all enjoyed our games. They've been exciting, and you've played with an eagerness that may have prolonged your lives. Does the old ticker good to get a jolt of excitement now and then. Several of you asked how you came to be chosen. Simple. I wanted top-notch competitors: successful, tough, creative, rich people. You're the cream of the crop."

"Moneywise I'm not in a league with the rest of you. Why me?"

Brent pointed at the speaker. "Have you all met Colonel Hahn, our token poor boy? Colonel, our money gains us access to classified data and high-level security areas. You've got something just as good, your military and CIA contacts. Besides, I'll bet you've already played a version of our game."

Hahn shrugged his shoulders, so Brent prompted, "Didn't you and your speak-five-language buddies ever get bored sitting around the campfire in Langley Virginia?"

"Sure, we polyglots sometimes got antsy."

"All that brilliance, all that testosterone, and you had to spend your days reading foreign newspapers for suspicious patterns. Didn't you ever stir something up just for fun?"

Hahn laughed, "Well, there was an uprising in Panama that I might have fomented just a tad."

Brent said, "Highway patrolmen have pools on who can ticket the most Chinese women, or baldies, or people driving red cars with Georgia plates. The need for action and competition is imprinted on the Y-chromosome."

He continued. "My assistant found lots of candidates. In this information age, even people like us can't hide much. I know how many times a day each of you takes a dump. Of the almost 2,000 potentials, you were the best. Our choices were vindicated, first, because everybody invited agreed to play; and second, by the videos you turned in."

Someone asked, "Will we get to see them?"

"Of course, that's why we're here. They document your successes. Most showed great creativity, though some of you should hire a good editor for the next round. Only one target didn't make it. Soto, the suicide was unfortunate, but we have to play the hand we're dealt. Next round you get first choice of targets, so things will even out. Dr. Hampton, in the future the three-hour video limit will be strictly enforced."

Hampton started to protest, but Brent motioned for quiet. "You're probably all wondering why you had to come to this dumpy place. That will become clear before very long. I'll just remind you that judges weigh esthetic factors heavily, and one such factor is careful timing of events."

Speech over, he inserted the first video into the VCR and turned off the lights.

First Date

Chez Panisse is located in what the locals affectionately call gourmet ghetto. All within seventy-five yards are two Thai restaurants, a Cambodian restaurant, a delicatessen, a South American restaurant, a coffee bar, a spectacularly good bakery, and an upscale supermarket. The jewel in the crown is Chez Panisse, a graceful brown shingle bungalow regularly ranked among the best restaurants in the U.S. Owner and chief chef Alice Waters and her staff pioneered California cuisine—healthy, fresh ingredients innovatively prepared. Paul had been intending to try it as soon as he inherited a gold mine. Marice gave him reason not to wait. But the friendly receptionist said that reservations for the fixed price meals must be made about a month in advance. Babe/Fyodor/Lancelot was undeterred. "Please, this is a very special occasion. Could I trouble you to call a few couples who have reservations. I'll give fifty dollars to anyone who'll let me go in their place tonight?" Ten minutes later he received a confirmatory phone call. He immediately made the next call, and she accepted the invitation. She insisted, however, that they meet at the restaurant.

Until London, Marice had grown to like most of her two dozen dates: A recently divorced fire captain who didn't want to go unaccompanied to a retirement ceremony. A shy computer specialist attending his sister's wedding. A star linebacker who ushered her onto an enormous yacht for a wild party with professional athletes and their gorgeous wives and girlfriends. During several occasions when they were briefly separated, other players rushed up to introduce themselves and scribble phone numbers or offer cards. She was never tempted, saying to each, "No thanks, I'm taken." Her date behaved like a gentleman. On the ride home she asked why she'd been needed. "You're a good-looking, famous athlete, you must have your pick of women."

He sighed, "I feel I can trust you. As a group, football players are much smarter than the brutish dolts the media make us out to be, but they're not especially enlightened. They're not ready to accept a gay man as a teammate. If they found out about me, they'd make my life hell."

She asked him to turn the car and drive to his hotel room. They talked throughout the night and fell asleep in each other's arms.

By her third date, Marice would have considering doing the job occasionally as a volunteer. It pleased her to help decent men without compromising her morals. But Paul Combes didn't fit the decent man profile. Despicable though he was, she'd have to spend the night pretending to be charmed. She hated pretense and wondered if she had any right to feel superior to him.

Promptly at 6:00, a taxi dropped Marice off in front of the restaurant. Paul, having arrived ten minutes earlier, sat on a bench holding a small pad and working on his poem. He put away the pad and extended his hand. "Hi Marice, I worried that you might not come."

She frowned, "I said I would. What were you doing?"

"Oh, just jotting down some thoughts. I have a neurotic need to be punctual, and other people don't, so I always carry a diversion. That way, waiting never bothers me."

"Well, I do get bothered. To me, 'fashionably late' is a synonym for rudeness."

Paul said, "One of my friends said he'd never wait more than five minutes for me. If I were that late, he'd start checking hospitals and the morgue."

She laughed excitedly. "My friend Toni said the same thing

just last week."

A young hostess ushered them through a commodious, softly lit room with vibrantly colored flowers decorating every table. Marice and a recent date had been led to an adjacent table by the same hostess. Marice signaled the hostess not to show recognition.

When they were comfortably seated, she breathed deeply. "Mmm, those smells are wonderful. This is so luxurious. Do you often treat first dates so nicely?"

"Usually we fly to Monte Carlo and then to the Sydney Opera House. But they're doing La Boheme and I've already heard it this year."

Marice stuck out her tongue. "And I thought I was special."

Paul said, "Actually, I haven't had many first dates lately. My most recent girlfriend and I decided almost simultaneously that we weren't lifetime material for each other. Since then I've led a pretty quiet single life."

The waiter arrived carrying warm frisée salad with house-cured ham and lardons. Marice folded, unfolded, refolded her napkin.

"Are you practicing for origami class?"

"Sorry, I'm just nervous. You said you're thirty-four. I'm surprised you never married."

"People shouldn't stay married if they fall out of love, but I want to be like my parents—married for forty years and in love till the day he died. So, I want to be sure and never have been."

(*I am superior to him, the lying bastard. He's talented, though. Even made himself tear up on cue.*) "Can anyone ever be sure?"

"Probably not. I've heard rumors that even some wrestling matches are fixed. Speaking of which, how do you and your 500-pound cronies keep busy when you're not tossing each other around the ring?"

"Have you heard of La Clínica de La Raza in Oakland?"

Paul hadn't. "Among other things, it's a clinic. I volunteered there during my senior year at UC, and when I graduated they offered me a real job. I counsel poor, pregnant women, mostly

Latinas although everybody is welcome. I help them get health services and give career advice. Many are drug abusers with serious medical conditions. Nobody else seems to care about them. I also teach bright high school and college students to tutor children. The job is perfect except for the pay."

Having decided to stick fairly close to the truth, she gave her correct age—twenty-five—and described growing up in a conservative Catholic home in South San Francisco with a younger sister. Her paternal grandmother had been black, and there were rumors of Cherokee blood. They were a tight-knit family.

Paul seemed excessively interested in her job and family. (*Figuring out my financial status*?) The man he claimed to be had grown up an only child almost a decade earlier and about 1,500 miles away in a rural area near Topeka. He shared many of her values. Like her, he was (claimed to be) crazy about kids, sports, ethnic restaurants, and movies. Like her, he didn't think much of opera, and hated cigarette smoke and Sean Hannity. (*Crazy, I have more in common with this bastard's pretend self than with any man I've known.*)

The waiter set down a gorgeous plate of Atlantic cod with anchovy oil and braised leeks. He uncorked a champagne bottle, but Marice held a hand over her glass. "None for me, thanks." Paul said, "Hey, you've got to have some. This bottle set me back five bucks."

Smiling wanly, she retracted the hand. "Just a taste." (*Can't lose control.)* Paul clinked glasses. "Here's to the start of a glorious relationship." She sipped. "It was worth every penny."

"Frankly, I can barely distinguish reds from whites. But I can tell bubbly from non, and this one comes highly recommended by the maître d'. I want tonight to be special."

He lied so effortlessly, she wondered about his capacity for greater sins. Even physical crimes. Rape, murder, mutilation. Serial killer Ted Bundy had also been handsome and charming. No reason to think that Brent would have forewarned her.

Marice heard snatches of conversation from other tables:

words like anamorphosis, verdure, neoclassical, didacticism. As during her previous visit, she imagined Chez Panisse patrons engaged in passionate debates about art and life in a Parisian café in the 1920s. The big one with the cigar in his pocket at the next table made her think of Hemingway, the baldhead could be Picasso. Paris in the'20s—Marice's image of utopia.

They cleansed their palates with Meyer lemon sorbet topped with red currant sauce. Paul dabbed a drop of currant sauce on his finger and touched it to her nose. She forced a smile.

"We grew currant in our back yard. They're yummy, but the plants have nasty thorns. My mom could never tell if it was blood or currant juice staining my brothers' clothes."

"Didn't know whether to spank or hug 'em, huh!"

Next came grilled Wolfe Farm quail in Banuyls vinegar sauce and a side of potato gnocchi with porcini mushrooms and chanterelles. Paul grinned, and Marice wrinkled her nose. "Is my red nose that amusing?"

"I'll bet the food here is as great as people say."

"Seems like you're in a good position to decide."

"That's what's funny. Movie stars and CEOs fly from all over the country to eat at Chez Panisse, and this may be my only chance. But I'm wasting it. You're too distracting. We might as well have gone to McDonalds."

"You're sweet," she said, and almost believed it.

They spooned up every drop of caramelized Bosc pears and crème fraîche ice cream. When Paul handed the waiter his VISA card, Marice insisted on leaving the tip. She watched him sign the bill, and then picked it up "to figure the proper amount." She walked toward the cashier. "I need change." She copied his VISA number on a piece of scrap paper.

They took the hostess's suggestion to walk upstairs for a breathtaking view of San Francisco Bay. As they stared out the large window, he put an arm around her shoulder. She gracefully extricated herself. Leaving, they walked up Shattuck, and Marice suggested that they stop at a nearby bookstore. Paul said, "That's where I always relax after a big Chez Panisse meal." She forced a smile. He asked, "Do you ever go on authors' nights, when they read from their own books?"

"Isabel Allende was wonderful. Maybe someday you'll be up there."

Paul squeezed her hand. She retracted it. They drifted to the local writers' section, and Paul found Leonard's *Black Shadow*. "I'd like to buy this for you. He's a friend of mine and needs the support, and I think you'll like it."

"Muchos gracias. Do you have any friends who make jewelry? There's an expensive store up the street."

While Paul waited at the checkout counter, Marice said she'd look around some more. Outside, she said "I bought you a present too." She lifted the book slowly from its sack until the title came into view—*How to Juggle*. They laughed together.

"My greatest accomplishment is not learning how to juggle. If I'd been any good, we might never have met."

They drove to a jazz club on University Avenue and listened to a sultry redhead accompanied by a guitarist, agreeing that she sounded like Nina Simone. At 1:15 the guitarist picked up his instrument while the vocalist crooned "Make it One for My Baby and One More for the Road." The busboy picked up their empty glasses. They were the last customers.

Paul said, "We can drive to your house, but it's such a beautiful night, if you don't live too far, let's walk."

"I've had a wonderful time Paul, but I'd rather take a cab."

For the first time that night, he frowned. "That's silly. Don't let my last memory of tonight be of you getting into a cab."

She relented—partially. "Alright, it is a nice night. My apartment is about a mile away on the Berkeley/Oakland border. But you've got to promise to turn back around when I tell you. I'm not ready yet to have you see where I live."

At Ashby she squeezed his hand and thanked him for the meal and book and entertainment—but pulled away when he bent to kiss her. "Please, let's not rush anything."

"Only if you promise to spend the rest of the night thinking about me. I know I'll be thinking about you."

None of Paul's dreams featured Babe Ruth or Fyodor Dosteovsky.

Marice often had trouble falling asleep, and on this night sleep proved extra difficult. Truck drivers rumbled through the street underneath her bedroom window, and two drunks got into a shouting match. The lumpy mattress made every position uncomfortable. Her eyes hurt and she couldn't concentrate on the new book. Her mind made a continuous loop of the events since Andronicos, without making sense of anything. Paul was charming and people seemed to like him, yet he was a fraud and lowlife. When she finally dozed off, her dreams, unlike Paul's, were not at all pleasant.

The phone jangled at 7:00. It was Brent—not her ideal wake-up call.

"Mornin' Chiquita, tell me all about it."

Legs crossed, needing the bathroom, "I did what you told me."

"And?"

"He was nice. We're going to see each other again tomorrow. Does that satisfy you?"

"I won't be satisfied until lover boy dumps his girlfriend and I get paid."

"Will you leave me alone after that?"

"Pretend I'm a big-time lettuce farmer, and I just paid off the guards to let you and all your cousins sneak across the border. Would I let you pick half a field and then send you back to Mexico? No, I'd keep you till you finished the job. I'll let you know when you've finished."

BACKGROUND CHECK

She cradled the phone, then changed her mind and dialed. Arturo sounded as sleepy as she had been moments earlier.

"Hi, it's Marice. I need you to do me a favor."

She sought him out as soon as she arrived at work. "Were you able to learn anything, Arturo?"

The La Raza computer wizard puffed out his narrow chest. "It took me all morning, but I found out all you need to know. I'm sure it's the right Paul Combes. He did two years in Folsom for sexual assault, and he walked on a second case when the alleged victim mysteriously refused to testify."

Marice buried her face in her hands. Brent hadn't lied. She'd been forewarned and had only herself to blame for her stupid romantic ideas.

Arturo's chest immediately receded. He pried her hands apart and kissed her cheek. "Oh cookie, I'm sorry. I thought he was a job applicant and I wanted to have a little fun. Combes got two parking tickets in the past five years and didn't vote in a recent election. Other than that, he's clean. He really is from Kansas, graduated from UK, no arrest record, no psychiatric history, never been married."

"Arturo, I've got to be sure."

"Baby, you offend me. You're dealing with an expert. If he had played hooky in the sixth grade, I'd know."

Marice hugged him. "Thanks honey, I love you."

"Then don't get involved with that gringo. You can have me."

Arturo was also the resident drug expert. Marice said, "I'm a nervous wreck. I need one more favor."

Cody's tickets for the sold-out Belafonte concert put them front-row center. The audience applauded continuously throughout the entire program and two encores. Belafonte left the stage drenched in perspiration. Afterwards, Paul and Marice drove to a coffee house on Ashby, not far from where he'd dropped her off the last time. She handed him a CD.

"My father went to Cuba last year and discovered a wonderful musical group. They call themselves the Buena Vista Social Club. I love their exuberance. He taped them, and I made a copy for you."

They walked, and she snuggled against him to stave off a brisk wind. Once again she insisted that he turn back short of her apartment, but this time she concluded the goodnights by reaching for his lips. The kiss lingered. Although it felt wonderful, she'd never been so confused.

The next morning Paul drove to Rasputin Records with the windows wide open, belting out the remembered words to "Jamaica Farewell" and humming the rest. He bought her two Belafonte albums. All that stood in the way of unqualified euphoria was a slight uneasiness about his incredible string of good fortune. He could rationalize the softball game. He was a good athlete and the other team had screwed up. The writing award wasn't too shocking. He'd submitted the story thinking it had possibilities, and his best friend had been a judge. But only sorcery could explain Marice. Lovely, charming, funny, smart, yet seemingly captivated by him. He wondered if anyone had ever won the lottery and the next day been hit by a bus.

ALIEN SQUIRRELS

THEY SPENT AT LEAST an hour on the phone for each of the next few days, and on the following Sunday drove through the Berkeley hills. Marice asked him to slow down as they approached a Julia Morgan designed home, and a little further on she pointed out a Maybeck. Paul had known that innovative architect-designed homes were scattered throughout the Berkeley area, but he'd never investigated. "Over there," she said, "was a gorgeous Maybeck—I've seen pictures—but the fire destroyed it." Berkeley's fire of 1991 had destroyed about 3,000 hillside homes. Towering eucalyptus and pines make the hills a place of majestic beauty, but the trees are filled with volatile oils. They literally exploded in the intense heat, and their charred stumps dominated the landscape. Many residents emigrated to safer areas. Others, wallets fattened by insurance settlements, replaced lost homes with even larger ones. New construction made the narrow, winding roads, so difficult for firefighters to navigate in 1991, even more inaccessible. Virtually no rain falls on the Bay Area from May through October, and the tall grasses and weeds become tinder. Hundreds of small brush fires flare up each year, leading experts to predict that another conflagration is inevitable and will cause unprecedented devastation.

Paul parked outside a locked gate with a sign: ANIMAL BEHAVIOR STATION. He'd borrowed the key from a UC faculty friend who worked at the research facility and said that it was usually deserted on Sunday afternoons. "C'mon, I'll show you the best views in the Bay Area. We'll have the whole place to ourselves." He locked the gate behind them. Just a short walk in and they could see the San Rafael Bridge fifteen miles to the north, the Dumbarton Bridge about forty miles south.

He offered her an apple from their basket, and she responded by unwrapping two brownies from her purse. "My friend Arturo made these with homegrown marijuana. No pesticides." Paul demurred "I couldn't get any higher than being here with you." Marice asked if he'd mind if she ate one. "No, except that when my friends smoke marijuana, they accuse me of becoming incredibly dull. Even though I'm probably no more dull than usual." She didn't mention that the brownie would be her first ever. Arturo had said he used marijuana as a calmative. She needed desperately to stay calm.

The cages of the small, private zoo housed spider monkeys, opossums, a mangy fox, and several unknown species of birds. Six spotted hyenas lived in a large, outdoor enclosure. All the animals were subjects in research projects. Marice noticed a small lizard sunning on a rock and tugged excitedly at Paul's shirt, then tiptoed very slowly to get close. Softly, "Can you see, Paul. His coat is iridescent. I wish we'd brought a camera." Later, she said, "Animals are so interesting when they're uncaged."

They spread an army blanket under a huge eucalyptus tree overlooking the bay, and she pointed to the sun streaking golden across the water. "It does that every day. That's why early settlers called California the golden state." He leaned back and cradled her head on his chest. The marijuana hadn't kicked in yet, but she felt peaceful. He said, "Thanks for the Buena Vista CD. I've played it five times already." He almost never sang with other people in earshot, but he began crooning "When I fall in love, it will be forever," and on the second time around she joined in. They sang duets, reveling in their mutual inability to carry a tune, improvising the lyrics as needed. He sang "Unforgettable, in every way." She improvised, "Then I guess I'll stay." She giggled at her witticism. The giggle turned into a full-fledged laugh that soon became uncontrollable and contagious.

Finally catching her breath, she lowered her voice in an

attempt to sound serious. "Tell me about your career as a subject. Did you really have your spinal fluid tapped?"

"Twice."

"What was the scariest thing you did?"

"I signed up for a brain scan experiment. After an hour, the technician unhooked me and handed me a check for $200. A week later, a second $200 check came in the mail. Turned out the experiment hadn't ended when I left. They had secretly followed me for days after. That happened two years ago. For all I know I'm still a subject."

"That's unethical."

"Maybe, but standard practice. A Harvard doctor documented dozens of unethical, government-approved medical experiments into the 1960s. A chemist at the University of Maryland recently documented a bunch of new ones. Researchers force schizophrenics to take drugs or withhold effective drugs just to see what will happen."

Marice said, "You're so brave."

"My friends say almost the same thing, only when they pronounce 'brave' it comes out 'idiotic.'"

"How about 'totally crazy?'"

"That's twice you've called me crazy. Starting today, I dedicate my life to making you fall in love with crazy."

"I'll consider myself warned."

Paul asked about a chip in one of Marice's front teeth, and she pretended to pout. "I've been trying not to smile so you wouldn't notice. I fell off a bike when I was eight and have been grim ever since." She gave her best grim look and he mimicked her. Each tried to make the other laugh first. His mouth twitched, she bit her lip to stifle a giggle, and they fell against each other guffawing.

She rubbed her finger across the scar below his right eye. "You've got no business making fun of me, Quasimodo."

"I earned this dueling scar defending the honor of an extraordinary woman." They fixed stares again, this time able to hold off the laughter for only seconds. "What actually happened is that some rednecks were hassling a dear friend of mine—the one who wrote the book I gave you—so I ran to his rescue. They beat the hell out of both of us."

"That's a scar to wear proudly. And you can tell your friend that he's a great writer. I loved the book."

He touched the chip. "I'm glad you've got a flaw. Maybe you're not a figment of my imagination."

Marice was experiencing a drifting, floating sensation. She snuggled closer. "Do you often worry about such things?"

"My big dream is to write a novel about useless stuff like the nature of reality. The idea that one's self is the only thing that's real is called solipsism. It fascinates me."

"So if you're a solipsist, where does that leave me?"

He kissed her forehead. "You're proof against solipsism. I can't even draw a decent stick figure, so I am surely incapable of creating Venus. But since we're discussing philosophy I'll deduct lunch as a business expense."

"Your imagination must be pretty good if you're a soon-to-be famous writer. Tell me about your stories."

"Mostly science fiction. Bizarre worlds, time travel. My favorite is a story about a man who travels back to what he'd always thought of as utopia, Paris of the 1920s, and eventually realizes that Berkeley of the 2020s can be equally exciting. I try to create lots of weird creatures. By the way, check out those squirrels."

Several small squirrels chattered in the nearby trees, and two brave ones made periodic ground forays for food. "My guess is that they're highly intelligent aliens, very possibly hostile. We may be in serious trouble."

She scrunched up her forehead, "Did you sneak a brownie?"

"Shh," he whispered. "They're watching for signs of weakness. If we lose contact with each other, they'll attack."

By now, Marice's giggles were bursting forth like daisies after a spring rain. She managed to say, "I don't think they've spotted us."

"Quick, hold me tight. That way, there'll be less of us to see."

She stuck out her tongue, exposing the chip. "They're probably harmless tourists. I'll bet you hired them to scare me." As she spoke, her arms reached out and encircled his waist.

"Better do exactly as I say. They haven't had a female for days, and they're ravenous."

She widened her eyes and gasped.

His index finger drew a line across her cheek. "My magic finger will protect you. Wherever it touches becomes invisible to them." The finger moved across her eyelids, tickled her ear, stroked her neck.

He stopped, sat up, pointed to a plump little guy running along a low branch. "That fiend saw us. He has a lip fetish. Nobody with unprotected lips is safe." Paul lowered his head until his lips protectively covered hers. Marice protected him back.

Carefully maintaining lip contact, they slid to the ground and lay motionless for several minutes. He gently kneaded her back and whispered, "Squirrels sometimes metamorphose. They become almost microscopic and snuggle into clothing. Should I check?"

In a moment of clarity, she rose upright. Fast easy sex was not her style. Besides, Arturo might have missed something, and Paul might really be a monster. The brownie had been a terrible idea. A woozy head was the last thing she needed.

The moment passed. Feeling incredibly sensuous and unwilling to risk being infested with metamorphosized alien squirrels, she lay back down on the blanket and stretched out. Paul knelt alongside to carefully scrutinize first her left shoe, then her right. Detecting no aliens, he asked next for her pants belt. She drew it slowly through the loopholes. Still, despite his thorough inspection, the invaders remained hidden. He recalled reading that they had an affinity for blouses. He lifted hers gently over her upraised arms, then stood back to admire flat stomach and large nipples outlined clearly under lacy white bra. She tousled her hair, and he softly whistled. "Hey," she admonished, "you're supposed to check the blouse, not me. And what if the aliens are in your clothes." With that, she motioned him to lift his arms. Raising herself to remove his tee shirt, she rubbed their chests together, slowly, languorously.

Pants, they both agreed, were an unlikely haven and quickly discarded. He was thankful, as his had become unbearably tight. Boxer shorts and panties came off more slowly. Then he realized they had miscalculated. The aliens were too clever to let themselves be found through visual inspection alone. So he began bare body, tactile reconnaissance, first cupping and squeezing well-formed breasts with his hands, then caressing her nipples with more sensitive lips and tongue while she traced fingernails across his back. His hand reached between her slightly parted legs and stroked her inner thigh. The furry triangle pointed to the aliens' most likely port of entry. One finger, then two, investigated and exited wet and sweet. No alien could have remained undetected for long.

Marice moaned softly, louder, louder still. And then—lottery winners met bus.

Venn Again

From behind a small thicket of Scotch Broom about twenty yards away emanated a man's voice, loud and thick with Brooklyn accent.

"Squirrels, my ass! Jesus Christ, Combes, you're supposed to be a creative genius. Is that the best you can do!"

The intruder emerged from the thicket, brushed himself off, and stared lasciviously at Marice. She rolled the blanket around her. He inhaled from a large cigar and casually blew a smoke ring. "Hello, ma'am, you are lovely. Please don't cover yourself on my behalf. My name is Venn. Colonel Aristotle Venn." Bronson Colfax's nemesis, Irving Edelman, would have identified the man as Doctor Venn.

Except for his scuffle a few weeks earlier with the idiots assaulting Leonard, Paul hadn't thrown a punch in anger since an epic battle with his best friend about twenty years earlier. But his heart that had pounded ecstatically just moments ago, now pounded with rage. Shouting, "Who the hell do you think you are," he cocked his fist and advanced. He would have felt more menacing with pants on. The interloper, about Paul's age, shorter and stockier, covered his mouth and yawned.

Marice leapt to her feet and the blanket slid off onto the ground. Ignoring her nakedness, she faced Venn, glowering, body quivering, fists clenched. Without warning, she threw back her head and screamed with the strength of an opera diva. Paul froze in mid-stride, and she picked up a jagged rock and held it aloft beside him. First one hyena, then all six, began to howl.

Although Venn directed his remarks at Paul, his eyes fixated on Marice. "My job has never been so enjoyable." He opened a hand to display a photo ID card, stamped CIA. "Please inspect my identification card and ensure yourself it's authentic."

Paul squeezed Marice's shoulder. He retrieved the blanket, handed it to her, and walked cautiously to Venn. The card looked official, but he knew that he could easily be fooled by anything more sophisticated than a Captain Marvel Junior Cadet Badge. To reassure Marice, he said, "I think this guy really is in the CIA." Marice suspected otherwise. She gritted her teeth and glared.

Venn dropped the accent. "Of course I'm in the agency. I try to make my introductions interesting. I hate the stereotype that we're all unimaginative and humorless." His eyes never blinked.

Paul said, "Turn around so my friend can get dressed. And I don't care who you are, you violated our rights. I expect an apology."

Venn seemed amused by the concept of boundaries on CIA behavior. But he covered his eyes and said, "If I've offended either of you, please accept my humblest apologies." His manner was distinctly unhumble. Then he asked a question so rich with strange implications that it made Paul shiver. "Will you do a simple task to help Marvin Flynn? Marvin, whose older brother is Lawrence."

Paul had played little league baseball with a Marv Flynn about twenty-five years earlier. Marv, who had an older brother named Lawrence. Never particularly close, they hadn't seen each other since their last game together. Paul formed a fuzzy mental picture of Marv and projected it forward a quarter of a century. Maybe, he thought, Marv had visited the Bay Area, heard his radio show by chance, and decided to play a practical joke. But try as he would, the image of Marv refused to evolve into the person before him. He mentally toured the whole team and stopped abruptly at center field. Relieved to make some sense of things, momentarily willing to ignore the terribly ill-timed interruption, he smiled and said, "I know you. Bobby Sherman, you son of a bitch." He extended his hand.

The man backed out of handshaking range. "My name is Venn.

CIA. Can I expect your cooperation in the matter concerning Marvin Flynn?" Now that Venn had exposed his zany, madcap side, he was all business.

Paul said, "I won't do anything without more information." Marice said, "Let's get out of here. Now." Certain that Brent had orchestrated the interruption, she was terrified for Paul's safety.

Venn cocked his head as though considering Paul's request. "National security is involved, but if you accompany me in my car, I'll tell you as much as permitted. This is a matter of great urgency."

Paul didn't consider himself a target for kidnapping. He had no wealthy relatives or access to state secrets. Unable to think of any plausible alternatives, he decided to temporarily accept Venn at face value. "But we have to take Marice home first."

"No can do. Have her drive your car."

"No," she screamed. "Don't go with him." Marice considered blurting out the details of her London trip. But, she realized, Venn must be armed if he had murderous intentions. Forcing his hand would be foolish.

She whispered, not completely truthfully, that the marijuana effect had dissipated and she could manage the short ride home. She promised to drive slowly and asked Paul to call as soon as Venn left. He reluctantly handed her the keys. She walked to the wide open gate and saw a black Mercedes parked next to Paul's Prius, a sheared off lock sitting near it on the ground. On a hunch, she wrote down the Mercedes' license number.

Paul also noted and memorized Venn's license number. He asked what kind of trouble Marv was in. "Life-threatening." Having divulged all he intended to, Venn lit a long, foul-smelling cigar. Paul asked him to extinguish it, and Venn answered, "A man's car is his surrogate castle." He puffed silently while Paul sullenly held his head out the window. Without asking directions, Venn drove directly to Paul's house, pulled into the driveway, and motioned his passenger to get out.

"How do I help Marvin?"

Venn reached to the back seat and picked up a small package

wrapped in ordinary brown paper. He said, "Deliver this to the address on front by midnight tonight. Don't be late and don't open it. For Marvin Flynn's sake." Before Paul could speak, Venn put a finger over his lips and drove off.

Coitus Uninterruptus

Marice's answering machine was blinking, indicating two messages. As soon as she pressed play, she cringed. Brent's voice. He started in without bothering to give his name. "So I lied about Paul. He's not the worst person on earth and isn't involved with another woman. He'll be safe as long as you don't tell him anything. Keep in mind that you never would have met him without me. You should be grateful."

She pressed again, hopeful that message number two would be more positive. But it was Brent again: "By the way, don't plan on whispering under the sheets. Now that Paul's been drafted into the CIA, we'll be giving him weekly lie detector tests. If he shows any knowledge of what's going on, he won't have to take the next test. He'll disappear. For that matter, we may occasionally test you."

The phone rang and she let the machine record again. Listening to Brent's messages was easier than having to actually speak with him. But it was Paul. She snatched up the receiver and prepared to do the acting job of her life. She assured him she'd made it home safely and listened while he described his ride. When he reached the part about choking on cigar smoke, she suggested they tie Venn up and throw him to the squirrels. Then she asked, "Why don't you come here. We can deliver the package together."

"Because, little stoned one, you have my car."

She said her trip home had been harder than anticipated, so she didn't want to drive to his place. He said he'd take a taxi.

Marice resolved to obey Brent to the letter of his law but to violate the spirit whenever possible. His henchman hadn't commanded her to deliver the package, so she tried on a succession of outfits to see which would be best for diverting Paul: tight skirt with low cut blouse, only semi-devastating; shorts and bra, much better. By the time the doorbell rang, she had changed to a teddy nightie—pink, silk, and sheer—and a perfume hinting of lemon blossoms. Paul stood motionless, staring as though he expected a beam of light to encircle and draw her heavenward. Hands on his cheeks, he stuttered, "You are the most gorgeous creature ever." He nuzzled her neck and let the fragrance fill his head while cheek and lips traced a path along her shoulder. "Mm," he sighed, "Citrus Marice. I love it."

Marice pointed to a bottle on the dresser affixed with a label: Paul, July, 2020. "I bought that yesterday and will never wear it again except to dab my wrist. Whenever I want to remember tonight, I'll take a smell."

"Oh, do you have something planned for tonight?"

The chip appeared. "There's a squirrel on the balcony. It's been watching me."

If she was overplaying the squirrel bit, Paul didn't mind. "We've got some unfinished business." So, with even greater diligence than previously, they renewed the search that had been interrupted in the hills. Either out of carelessness or because they believed the aliens deaf, they made no attempt to suppress their sounds of pleasure. This time, an additional probe supplemented his hands and mouth. The new tool, not purely for reconnaissance, eventually discharged wave upon wave of long-tailed swimmers inside her. The accompanying sounds would have alerted all but the most severely hearing-impaired intruders. Fifteen minutes later, a second amphibious assault launched a new wave of kamikaze swimmers, tails waggling happily until the end.

The clock read 10:00. "Venn said the package must be delivered by midnight. I'm not sure what to do."

"Venn's a creep."

"He's probably laughing about this right now."

"Then don't go. Stay with me."

"I've got to. If anything happened because I hadn't done this piddly thing, I couldn't live with myself." He kissed her. "The address is in north Berkeley. It shouldn't take more than a half-hour."

She asked him to wait while she got dressed, but he insisted on going alone. He worried that the small package contained an illicit drug or microdots of confidential information. Beyond that, his imagination failed. She turned on the radio and said she'd wait up. Thoughts turning to London, she huddled inside a blanket.

Feeling simultaneously silly and scared about the possibility of becoming a serious lawbreaker, Paul took the stairs two at a time and ran to where she'd parked. The car sat strangely low, and when he got close the reason became obvious. Someone had slashed all four tires. He climbed inside and dispiritedly tried the ignition. The engine turned over as usual. He jumped out and ran back to her apartment. Gasping for breath, he banged on the door and called out, "Marice, I've got to take your car. Where are the keys?"

She held a balled-up roll of tissues to reddened eyes.

"What's wrong?"

"I'm okay," she said, smile and tears fighting to control her face.

He massaged her shoulders, "C'mon, talk to me."

She wished she could tell the truth. "It's silly. You had to leave."

"You know I did."

"You must think I'm a wild woman. Marijuana brownies, casual sex." She sniffled, every bit as miserable as she was acting, though not for the reasons implied.

"I knew all along what kind of woman you are. Remember that guy in the produce department at Andronicus. He's my buddy. We tip each other off when we see women in desperate need of sex."

Marice dabbed her eyes. Paul's attempt to lighten the mood having fallen flat, he squeezed himself against her. "It wasn't casual for me."

"Everything seemed so perfect, then you had to go. We didn't even have time for an after-sex cigarette. Wham, bam, thank you ma'am." Pointing to the Beatles posters that covered the extra bedroom wall, she said, "I've been a Beatles fan since I was eleven. Paul was always my favorite."

"Remember that softball game in Golden Gate Park?" She nodded. "I was embarrassed that a dumb game made that day one of the happiest of my life." He stroked her hair. "Every day since has been a hundred times better."

She kissed his chest. Shrugging her shoulders, she let the bathrobe covering the nightie slither to the floor. He caressed her buttocks, reached under her knees, and lifted and carried her to the bed. She put her arms around his neck and held tightly. "Please," she said, "don't go. Don't leave me for another minute."

He began unbuttoning his pants. "My duty as a gentleman is to stay. But don't think I enjoy any of this." She smiled, and smashed him with a pillow.

When the sex ended they lay together, arms entwined—Marice terrified, joyful, conflicted beyond belief, and Paul feeling unqualified bliss. After awhile his breathing slowed, and she heard the gentle rhythm of his respirations. Unable to sleep, she murmured his name. When he didn't respond, she extricated herself from his grip and took the phone into the bathroom.

"Hermanita," she whispered.

"Eece, what's wrong? It's 3:00 A.M."

"Sorry honey, I couldn't wait. I don't know what to do. He's wonderful, but we can't have a normal relationship. If I tell him anything, they might kill him." She recounted the events of the day. Thirty minutes later, she agreed to follow what seemed to both of them the only logical course of action: Act naturally, give Paul support, under no circumstances tell him about Brent. She'd be like a mother told her only child has a fatal disease. Hide the news from him, search for a cure, and try to make his remaining days joyful.

The morning light slithered through Paul's closed eyelids, and he dreamily reached across the bed. No Marice, just rumpled sheet. She'd spent the early morning riffling aimlessly through old magazines while trying unsuccessfully to devise a more proactive plan. She heard him stir, poured a cup of coffee, and started to place it on the nightstand. First she had to lift the small, undelivered package. He opened his eyes and smiled beatifically, then saw what she was holding. He took it from her and snapped the flimsy string. Inside, a small balsa wood plaque proclaimed:

> DOUBT IS NOT A PLEASANT CONDITION, BUT CERTAINTY IS AN ABSURD ONE. Voltaire

He saved the wrapper with the address and tossed the plaque in the waste basket.

Paul normally worked at home on Mondays. No unexpected crises had arisen at La Raza over the weekend, so Marice took a vacation day. They drove along the coast to explore Monterey and vicinity.

Holding hands on a cliff at Big Sur, salty wind whipping against them, they huddled 800 feet above the ocean to watch waves cascade relentlessly against rocks. Water against rock, an eons-long battle, and water always won. They descended a steep trail and during the frequent rest stops dropped bread crumbs to attract birds. She identified each species for him. At bottom, they picked their way among the protected tidepools of Pacific Grove. In Los Padres National Forest, Marice announced that she had an obsession about finding a heart-shaped rock whenever she traveled. They looked diligently and within an hour found three. She discerned slight imperfections in each. After the third rejection, he tapped her tooth and said, "How can you, of all people, be so intolerant of imperfections." She threw a half-eaten nectarine at him. It splattered on his chest and they wrestled, laughing, to the ground squishing the pulp evenly between them. Later he found a heart-shaped piece of feldspar that she proclaimed perfect.

Just before turning back, they glimpsed a female wild boar

with two young ones. Nature's bounty was limitless, but the topography and flora and fauna, like the food at Chez Panisse, barely mattered to Paul as long as Marice romped alongside. For her, the day evoked memories of Brent's aquarium.

Death of a Salesman

Paul's guest the next day was a game and puzzle expert who had recently won a cryptic crossword championship. She explained to the audience that cryptics don't rely on arcane bits of knowledge like the name of Disraeli's successor or the third largest river in South America. They require mental agility. One part of each clue means the same as the answer and can come anywhere within the clue. The other part is an anagram, pun, or similar device that leads to the answer. She gave examples:

If you are without pity, give less to her. 4 letters.

'Ruthless' means 'without pity' and is the result of adding 'less' to 'ruth.' The answer is Ruth.

Explore similarities and differences with mixed up chief executive officer covering broken ramp. 7 letters.

'Mixed up' indicates an anagram of chief executive officer (CEO) and it covers (is outside of) an anagram of ramp. ceo + ramp = compare (explore similarities and differences)

Extremes of manly possessive. 2 letters.

The letters at the extremes of 'manly' are m and y. The answer is my—a possessive.

Paul took an immediate liking to cryptics. The guest gave him an autographed copy of her recently published cryptic collection, and on the ride home he worked out:

His daughter gave birth to a thousand, padre. 11 letters

"His daughter gave birth" implies 'grandfather.' So does 'a thousand' (grand) + 'padre' (father). The answer is 'grandfather.'

and

Five digits sound like correcting penmanship. 11 letters

Five digits comprise a hand. A synonym for "correcting" is "righting," which sounds like "writing." So, the answer is 'handwriting,' which is a synonym for penmanship..

Bus forgotten, lottery winner of the century with two nights of lost sleep to recoup, he returned home for an early bedtime. The mailbox contained letters from a former station intern who had emigrated to New Zealand and a friend touring Kenya. Gus, the KDJM night janitor, took great pride in his stamp collection, so Paul scissored around the unusual stamps and dropped them in an envelope. Before opening the rest of the mail, he called to invite his mother for Sunday dinner to meet Marice. He barely glanced at a political mailer and supermarket flyer before tossing them into the bin for recycling. Then he opened a small brown envelope with no return address and shook out a five-line newspaper clipping inside. The clipping, from the Monday *Hartford Courant*, reported that thirty-four-year-old local citizen and rare coin salesman Marvin Flynn had been found dead under suspicious circumstances. Authorities had not ruled out foul play. Survivors included a wife and two young children.

Two-year-old Colombo sidled up and rubbed Paul's leg, which his so-called master correctly interpreted as more command than greeting. He hadn't eaten since morning, wanted food now, and meowed indignantly at Paul's lack of haste. The vet had given orders to put Colombo on a diet, but the vet hadn't been around during times of famine. So, as the sun sank low, his lackey dutifully mashed a can of turkey and giblets on the cat dish. He watered two philodendrons that had flourished during their six-month house residence, their hardiness the reason rather than any greenness of his thumb.

He reread the clipping, but the name Marvin Flynn and the word dead remained conjoined in the same sentence. He dabbed his eyes, poured a shot of brandy, and sank with queasy stomach into the sofa. Colombo jumped onto his lap to luxuriate, and Paul mechanically stroked the long, gray fur.

The room darkened. Paul sat silently and still. Finally, in complete blackness, he lifted Colombo off his lap and reached for the phone. When Marice regained control of her voice, she said the clipping must be fake and volunteered to contact the *Courant* to verify. She copied down the details and dutifully dialed. But she harbored little doubt.

Paul opened the *Chronicle*. The Giants and A's had both lost the previous day, stale news that he'd known the previous night. He used the bathroom, keeping the door ajar so he'd hear the phone. He slid a catnip-filled sock along the floor and watched Colombo bat it around. His watch read 9:00, meaning midnight in Connecticut. Assuming that most of the *Courant* staff had gone for the day, he expected a long wait. Keeping one hand on the phone, he sagged into the chair and closed his weary eyes.

Marice had no trouble getting through. She said she was calling to verify a news item, and the voice at the other end asked for the reporter's name. She was in luck—he had just walked into his office. The reporter verified the item's accuracy. There had been a suspicious death and he'd seen the body and talked to witnesses. The victim, without question, was thirty-four-year-old Kansas-born Marvin Flynn.

Marice's call jolted Paul like a shrill alarm clock at dawn. Pulse racing, he answered on the first ring and knew immediately from her tone, before his brain registered any actual words, that the clipping was genuine. Someone 3,000 miles away, an old teammate, had died. A man who never would have reentered Paul's consciousness except for the circumstances surrounding his death. And Paul bore responsibility.

Paul had interviewed victims of violent crimes and one perpetrator, but he'd never felt such a direct link to violence. After awhile his sadness and guilt became comingled with a sense of dread. Whatever the explanation for Marv's death, Paul guessed that he, Paul, knew too much. Marice had called him brave;

thankfully, she couldn't mindread. None of that mattered. He had to do something, to not would be immoral. He decided to file a police report, and when he called to tell Marice, she insisted on accompanying him.

They drove to the Oakland station. Although only fifteen minutes from the hills by car, parts of the downtown area had more in common with Bangladesh. Despite a temperate climate and proximity to San Francisco, few tourists visited. The streets after dark belonged to drug buyers and sellers, sex buyers and sellers, and people whose only bed was the sidewalk. The Chamber of Commerce hailed Oakland as the most integrated city in the U.S., with tremendous ethnic diversity. But hill properties were largely white-owned; in the flatlands, African-Americans, Latinos, and East Asians lived in separate ghettoes. Many occupied buildings damaged by the 1989 earthquake and then abandoned.

Paul let Marice out in front of the station. He found a parking space three blocks away and jogged through the war zone to the gray, concrete building. They joined up in the lobby and held hands until a desk officer acknowledged them. Paul whispered that they wanted to report a serious crime, so she put down her magazine and repeated the question she'd already asked more than a dozen times that night: "What is the nature of the crime?" The room quieted as others paused from filling out forms or waiting to be called and strained to hear the answer. He said softly, so as not to attract attention, "I think there's been a murder." She bellowed, "Do you think there's a body, and if so where do you think it's at?"

"Hartford, Connecticut."

She flipped the pen in the air and watched it drop. "That's out of our district, sonny."

Marice clasped Paul's hand. "We're together. Please get a police officer so we can explain."

The desk officer yawned. "You mean this is a long story."

Sneering, "Sure, I'll get our star detective." She dialed and spoke into the receiver as Watson to Holmes, "Are you free to do an intake interview? There's a couple here with a horrible tale of murder and mayhem." To the couple, "Captain Steige will be down shortly."

The captain, a tall, heavy-set man at the far end of middle age, did not stir visions of Holmes. His rumpled jacket reeked of alcohol, and he wobbled and slurred his speech. He led them up two flights of stairs to a windowless room better suited for grilling suspected felons than questioning volunteer witnesses. Closing the door, he bowed theatrically and said, "Captain James Robert Steige at your service. Please honor me by telling your story."

Marice considered and quickly rejected the idea of starting the narrative in London. She began with Venn's appearance in the park. Steige carefully wrote down the time and place, then asked if they could remember Venn's precise opening words. She answered truthfully and to her immediate regret. Steige scrunched up his face and pretended to search for deep meanings in "Squirrels, my ass." Careful not to repeat the mistake, she told a much bowdlerized version of their day in the hills. The censored parts might have held his interest, but their story of harassment by a possible murderer didn't. On the other hand, an open button on Marice's blouse riveted his attention. Steige's eye-movements and pupil size tracked her shifts in position with unerring diligence. When Paul said that he and Marvin had played baseball together, Steige interrupted to say that he'd been captain of his high school football team. He rolled up a sleeve and walked toward Marice. "I'm still in great shape, huh. Feel my biceps." Retired policeman Steige had earned the right to ham things up by his solid performance in the Edelman/poison oak drama. Marice, although baffled by the mechanism, inferred a Brent/Steige connection and became prudently quiet. Paul, on the other hand, assumed that rudeness and incompetence were standard operating procedure for the Oakland police department. He intended to have none of it.

"We're here to talk about a murder. If you can't help, please find someone who can." Steige's demeanor changed to unctuously polite. He called downstairs for coffees and asked them to get comfortable while he left to gather information. Marice pleaded with Paul to leave, but he insisted on seeing things through. Steige returned forty-five minutes later, this time sober and respectful. He said that the CIA had vouched for Venn. He refused to say more other than that they should forget the name Marvin Flynn.

Paul might have accepted such an edict earlier, but the shabby treatment had incensed him. When Steige opened the door to usher them out, he said, "Let's find a decent law enforcement person to tell my radio audience how this should have been handled." They reached the lobby, Steige trailing a few steps back, just as two *Tribune* reporters entered the station. Unwilling to ignore the apparent sign of divine intervention, Paul shouted: "I'm a citizen and have a right to be treated as such." His voice boomed throughout the station. Steige caught up and draped a restraining arm on Paul's shoulder. "Calm down, old buddy." Paul knocked off the arm and beckoned the reporters. But, recent baseball superstardom notwithstanding, they didn't recognize him and assumed he was working off a drunk. On urgent business, they never slowed down.

Having so forcefully asserted his rights, Paul refused to be herded sheep-like outside. He sat down on the cold, tiled floor and announced, "I'm not leaving till you handle my complaint properly."

Steige waved for two policemen. They dragged him toward a holding cell while two others kept Marice at bay. A drunk in the waiting room shouted "Police brutality" and whistled and stamped his feet encouragingly when Paul momentarily broke free.

The cell door clanged shut. Steige came by to say that disorderly conduct charges would not be filed and Paul would be released after he'd been calm for an hour. He urged Paul to forget about Venn and Flynn. Marice waited for Steige to come back up front. She said, "Tell Brent that if anything happens to Paul, I'll find a way to kill him." Steige smiled avuncularly. "It's unwise to announce homicidal intentions in a police department."

At 2:00 A.M. a polite young policeman unlocked the cell door and told Paul he could go. He volunteered the information that Marice had been driven home. Paul jotted down the time, wanting accurate facts for the complaint he'd file after catching up on sleep. He trudged to the car, temples pounding, throat and stomach engorged with acid, and sped through the deserted streets.

The causes of Paul's distress were somewhat abstract: death of a barely remembered acquaintance, unprofessional cop, weird and possibly fraudulent CIA man. By contrast, Marice's misery had a palpable, extensive, and terrifying basis—intensified by Brent's order that she deceive Paul. She flopped onto bed, resisting the urge to once again wake Joanna. She put on one of her new Belafonte albums and lay awake until long after it stopped playing.

POTENTIAL VICTIM NUMBER 2

THE LIGHT FROM A street lamp revealed a man on his front porch, peering through the living room window. Presuming he'd surprised a burglar, Paul slowed down and turned on the brights. The man turned slightly but stood his ground. Paul opened the glove box and felt for a wrench—not much help if the man carried a gun. He regretted not having his cell phone. Every muscle taut, gripping the wrench tightly, he swerved into the driveway. The man turned full face and gave a familiar leer. Venn greeted him as nonchalantly as a friend meeting for an after-work drink.

Paul sputtered, "This is private property. Get off."

"Or what? Will you sic your police department pals on me?" He held out an envelope. "Hand this to your old flame Donna Brookens by noon tomorrow."

Paul and Donna had dated for awhile and become friends: monthly phone calls, Christmas cards, occasional lunches. They had taken unsuccessful turns playing matchmaker for each other. Venn's mention of Donna made the web of mystery more intimate and frightening.

"Are you threatening Donna?"

Venn touched the middle and forefingers of his right hand to his forehead and gazed silently upward, then turned and trotted away. Paul took a few tentative steps forward but realized the futility of giving chase. Suppressing a shout that would have alarmed sleeping neighbors, he stood helplessly with hands on hips and watched Venn disappear around a corner.

No reason to wake Donna at 3:00 A.M. The call could wait till morning. He set the alarm for 7:00 and slept fitfully, waking with a headache that resisted two aspirins and a hot shower. Feeling very uncomfortable, he dialed.

"Hello."

"Hi Donna, it's Paul Combes."

"Paul! Strange time for a call. Is everything okay "

"Something crazy happened that may involve you. Let me explain."

"Okay, but I have to leave for work in twenty minutes."

"A few days ago a man with a CIA badge asked me to deliver a package for the sake of an old friend. I didn't. Soon after, the friend died unexpectedly under suspicious circumstances. The police confirmed that the CIA connection is real. Last night, the man came to my house with an envelope and said I should get it to you by noon today."

Donna giggled. "Paul, if you're desperate to see me, just say so."

"I'm serious."

Long pause. "How did your friend die?"

"The paper said that foul play is a possibility."

"You're scaring me."

"Tell me where I can hand you the envelope."

"I have to meet a client and we'll probably be together all morning."

"Please, just tell me where you'll be. It's dumb, and I feel like an idiot, but I don't want you on my conscience."

"I should always be on your conscience. Paul, you mean well and you're the sweetest person I know, but he's an important client. I can't have my business interrupted."

"Donna, please."

"Gotta go. Call me tonight. I'd love to see you." Click.

Paul redialed and let the phone ring eight times before slamming it down. The answering machine at her graphic design firm reported a 9:00 A.M. opening time, so he took another aspirin and waited. The receptionist refused to divulge Donna's client's address. Paul pleaded, calling it literally a matter of life and death, until she finally relented and connected him with her boss. The boss couldn't help, as Donna hadn't told anyone her schedule. Paul asked for a list of Donna's clients, and the boss invited him to the office. The receptionist handed him a sheet containing sixty-five names and phone numbers. "Mr. Deane said you could sit at that desk." Paul called every number, dialing and redialing for more than an hour under the receptionist's suspicious eyes, but nobody acknowledged a morning appointment with Donna Brookens.

He stared at his watch: 10:15, 10:16, 10:17. The Oakland phone book had no listing for Central Intelligence Agency but San Francisco's did, under government offices. The receptionist said that no agent named Venn was available.

"Do you have an agent named Venn?"

"That is confidential information."

He explained what ostensible agent Venn had asked him to do and Marvin's death and the threat to Donna. The voice at the other end said that somebody must be playing a joke. When he persisted, the voice said that she could divulge no more information. 10:22.

He called information for each Bay Area city and asked for all listings for Venn. He called all nine. No luck. 10:37.

A mutual friend found a number for Donna's sister in Menlo Park. He asked if she had any idea who Donna might be meeting that morning. She didn't. 10:44.

He tore open the not-to-be-delivered envelope. Inside, an ordinary white card contained the words: A TRUE REALIST DEMANDS THE IMPOSSIBLE. He ripped it into tiny pieces. 10:45.

He returned home, fed Colombo, and stared at his picture of Donna posing in a yellow sundress by the Lake Merritt boathouse. 11:45. The all-news radio station gave no reports of a Bay Area death. Marice called and he told her what had happened. She said she'd come by after work.

The phone rang at 2:20, but Paul didn't pick up. Donna wouldn't be calling, and nobody else mattered. The answering machine came on but the caller didn't leave a message. After three minutes of silence, the ringing started anew followed by another brief hiatus and then four more rings. When the next series started, he wiped sweaty palm on pants leg and pulled the receiver to his ear.

Venn, without a hello, "That's two on your head. You'll read about it tomorrow. I hope you plan to save your girlfriend."

Paul covered the mouthpiece and sobbed for the first time since his father's funeral. Then he grabbed the phone and screamed, "You miserable bastard." Almost immediately, the scream turned to a whimper. "Please, don't hurt Marice." Venn said, "Whatever you're thinking, get it through your head that I'm on your side."

"Two people are dead. Why? Tell me why."

"I'd like to chat but there's work to do. So, what'll it be? Ignore my instructions or try to save her."

Paul whispered that he'd do whatever Venn wanted. He was told to go to the main gate at Treasure Island. Situated midway between Oakland and San Francisco, Treasure Island had been a military installation before being converted to civilian use. Some military presence remained. Commanding spectacular views of the bay and both cities, it was a prime piece of real estate.

TREASURE ISLAND

PAUL TOOK THE TREASURE Island exit off the Bay Bridge. At a sentry booth, he explained that he had an appointment. The sentry glanced at his driver's license, scanned a sheet, and handed back the license. "Sorry sir, I have no listing here for a Combes or Venn. I'm afraid you'll have to—"

Before he completed the sentence, a black limousine pulled up and the driver called out, "I'll take over." The sentry saluted briskly and stepped aside. Paul switched cars and was driven to a small stone building with a sign on the entryway: AUTHORIZED PERSONNEL ONLY. As soon as the driver announced their presence into an intercom, a second man materialized to guide Paul down a hallway. He knocked at a sturdy iron door and marched off, leaving Paul to stare ahead bewildered.

The door slid open. A hot vapor oozed out and Paul instinctively retreated into the hallway, covering his nose. The door opened further to reveal Venn, naked, feet dangling in a hot tub, remote control device pointed at the door, cigar protruding from grinning mouth.

"Come in, sit down, dip your feet." He tossed a can toward Paul. "Have a coke. We've got a lot to do."

Paul put the can by his feet. "Get started. You know why I'm here."

"Right, you want to keep honeypot safe. And to find out why your previously drab life has become so exciting. I don't suppose it matters that you'll be helping your country."

"Maybe you haven't heard. The Evil Red Empire collapsed.

We're all friends now."

"Yeah, all friends. And Madonna's a virgin." Into an intercom: "Harry, I'll have an iced coffee. Better bring a pitcher and two glasses and some sandwiches." He raised out of the water and farted.

"Hal Shinkman invited you to a couple of get-togethers. You didn't go. Don't look pissed off, we bugged his phone, not yours. I want you to call and say you'd like to be friends."

"Whatever you say. Just, please, don't let anything happen to Marice." Paul's long-sleeved shirt and Levis clung uncomfortably while sweat pooled inside his shoes.

Paul had met Hal in an advanced data analysis course at NYU grad school. The seven students who finished from an initial cohort of twenty had developed a sense of solidarity, and then he and Hal had both emigrated to the Bay Area. Paul had politely declined Hal's attempts to renew the relationship.

"You think you're too good for him. He's an ungainly slob who wears filthy clothes and has disgusting body odor. He's not in your league intellectually—you did much better than him in that course at NYU."

"I can't imagine how or why you know so much about me, but you're wrong about my reasons for not being friends. Hal's okay. We just went in different directions."

Venn rolled the cigar around his mouth. "Yeah, his was up. Imagine this. Smelly, stupid Hal is ten times more competent than you. He heads a spy ring that has seriously compromised this country's security. We know it but don't have enough evidence to convict."

An image flashed through Paul's mind of short, ectomorphic Hal swaddled in a long trench coat, twirling a combination cigarette case/pistol, attached by each arm to a gorgeous, naked woman. He couldn't help himself—despite his awful predicament, he laughed aloud.

Venn shook his head disgustedly and clicked the remote. A private marched in with drinks and sandwiches. Paul removed his dripping shirt and accepted an iced coffee.

"The way I see it, Shinkman would have turned you eventually. Your file is an embarrassment."

"File? On me? I don't believe you."

Face flushed, he leaned against a wall. Venn drummed his fingers against the side of the hot tub.

"Okay, maybe the CIA has a file on me and everybody else with black friends who likes peace and believes that gays and migrant workers are human. So what?"

"Remind me to kick your ass when we're done with this business. For now, thank me. I'm probably saving you from treason."

"Look, I'll play your paranoid game. Marice means too much, and I would have done it for Marv or Donna or anybody else. But I don't believe you about Hal Shinkman. Hal is the least likely spy imaginable. He's slow, boring, and uncoordinated, and nobody's going to hand him secret documents."

Venn slammed his hand against the hot tub. "Damn, you're dumb. I should get extra pay for working with civilians. You think all spies look like Sean Connery in his prime and drink double martinis, shaken, not stirred?"

"All I care about is Marice's safety, so let's get on with it."

"Okay, listen good. Lucky for you I'm your mentor, 'cause I'm the best spy-catcher in the business. Why? I don't use suave agents who look like they can bench press 500 pounds. I take Shinkman types. Their friends would swear they couldn't do anything requiring brains or skill or guts. Then, even if they get caught, allowances are made."

"But ossifer, I dint know this here place wuz jes fer soldiers. I thot it might be mighty fine fer huntin. Hope I dint inconvenience no-one."

"I guarantee you, Shinkman's effective and deadly. Hell, you'd need five years training to get into his league."

"Thanks for the vote of confidence. Did he kill Marv and Donna? If so, I'm in."

Venn leaned back puffing away as casually as a vacationer on a cruise ship, then whispered into a cell phone. Finally he turned to Paul. "Of course you're in. Make contact with Shinkman. Ingratiate yourself. After that, we'll figure out your next step. And don't ever question or threaten me. You've been drafted, I give the orders, and I won't tolerate insubordination. By the way, you will be paid."

Paul clicked his heels and saluted. "Jawohl, mein commandant. But I don't believe that Hal Shinkman is a spy and I don't want your damned money. Just leave Marice alone."

"You've been warned." To the guard at the door, "There's a sack labeled "OC" with some books and papers on my desk. Give it to Agent Combes." He closed his eyes and submerged himself in the water, terminating the interview.

If Paul had anticipated titles like *My Life as a Spy* and *CIA Diary*, or the latest on cryptography and telephone tapping, he was disappointed. The bulging sack contained three old books—*Mimicry*, *Adaptive Coloration in Animals*, and *Bioethics*—and a stack of notes, newspaper clippings, and pages ripped from magazines. Paul glanced at a page.

OC

When a mother killdeer spots a fox approaching her nest, she hops around pretending to be hurt. The fox pursues and gets close, but she keeps escaping at the last instant. When she's lured the fox a safe distance from the nest, she flies off.

A gorilla in the Basel zoo faked injuries so her keeper would stay close. On one occasion she pretended to have her hand caught between the cage bars. When the keeper rushed to the scene, the hand embraced and held her tight.

Some insects have an inconspicuous head and a detachable tail that looks like a head. A predator that strikes at the false head allows its intended victim to escape.

The scorpionfish's deep red dorsal fin sways from side to side while the rest of the scorpionfish lies motionless and camouflaged. An enlarged black spot on the fin gives the appearance of an eye, and a notch opens and closes like the mouth of a much smaller fish. Eager predators approach and become easy prey.

The bee martin, a Mexican bird, ruffs its head feathers so they look like a flower. Honey bees crawl inside and are eaten.

Confirmation

The local news section of the *Chronicle* reported a five-car pile-up on 101 South that had left one woman dead and three people injured. The dead woman was identified as Donna Broo-kens of Oakland.

ACT NATURAL

MARICE'S INSTRUCTIONS WERE MUCH simpler than Paul's. Act naturally, continue showing up for work, do your job efficiently, tell nobody but Joanna. She smiled a lot knowing that, at any moment, a spear might zoom upward from the bottom of the aquarium.

Glamor Girl Hal

Lesotho is a small African nation completely surrounded by South Africa. Piedmont is a small California city completely surrounded by Oakland. There the similarities end. Impoverished and disease-ridden Lesotho stands in sad contrast to white South Africa, whereas Piedmont is a wealthy oasis in the midst of Oakland's crime. Hal lived in upper Piedmont, where annual per capita income averaged about $100,000 more than in Paul's neighborhood. He seemed delighted by the call and invited Paul to join him and a few friends the next afternoon.

Three colors of flowering maples lined the long, curvy driveway. Paul squeezed the Prius between a late-model town car and a Jaguar still bearing the dealer's license plate. Bottle of merlot in hand he rang the doorbell, activating a recording of 100 decibels of Joel Grey welcoming pleasure-seekers to the Cabaret. The neighbors must have hated when visitors called on Hal. Not particularly impressive-looking from the street, the house was massive inside.

"Hi handsome, so glad you could make it. Come in, come in."

Despite everything preceding, the creature swaying lasciviously in the doorway caught Paul unprepared. Unmistakably Hal Shinkman, he wore an off-shoulder black dress slit to the thigh, a long blonde wig, and a halo of jasmine. On Marice the effect would have been stunning. But Hal looked less like a female impersonator than a comedian parodying female impersonators. Paul kept a straight face, though it took considerable effort.

He held out the wine. "Hello, Hal, good to see you."

Throaty, attempted femme-fatale voice: "I call myself Helena now. Don't stand there gaping. Do you like my new look?"

"I'm floored. It will take getting used to."

"Well, it's your own fault, sweetie. I invited you to my coming out party last year. Tell me, why did you call after all this time?" Hal winked. "Are you lonely?"

Paul said he had been commissioned to put together a show featuring eastern transplants to the Bay Area. Hal/Helena pouted, "I'd hoped it was more personal. Let's go downstairs." He took Paul's reluctant hand and led the way past a punchbowl filled with assorted pills, vials, needles, and cigarettes. "Please, help yourself."

Celebrants packed the spacious, brightly lit basement. Hal and his provocative outfit, though as ill matched as fingernails and blackboards, would have received challenges from several guests in a competition for most bizarre. A man dressed in rags lay on the floor next to a shopping cart full of newspapers, rags, and bottles. Another wore two water-filled transparent sacs as breasts, with a goldfish swimming in each. A woman painted a picture of a naked man while he pretended to be copulating with a stuffed sheep.

Somebody called and Hal flounced off, leaving Paul momentarily alone. A tall woman wearing only a black leather belt and scarf, with assorted candies dangling from both, slithered over. "Hungry? Help yourself," she invited. "Just drop twenty dollars in the can there. It goes to United Way." She pointed to a man a few yards away with a bunch of grapes decorating his crotch. "Or, if you prefer eating fruits..."

The invitation, directed at Paul, was accepted by a man standing nearby. He bit at a licorice strip that ended just below her left breast, chewing slowly and carefully until he'd exposed the nipple. With a piece of licorice strip still in his mouth, he stroked the nipple with his tongue. She held his head while winking at Paul. "Pretty wild outfit you're wearing."

"Thanks," he laughed, looking down at his Dockers and short-sleeved shirt. "I made it specially for this party."

The man moved his hand along her thigh. She pushed him away. To Paul, "Interested? You can forget the twenty dollars."

"Two weeks ago, I wouldn't have hesitated. But I just met a very special woman. You look so good, I'd go on a sugar binge that wouldn't be fair to anyone. So I'd better say no."

"Thanks for your honesty. Actually, Helena asked me to show you around. Hi Paul, I'm Candy. Shall we tour the house?"

He welcomed the opportunity to spy on the so-called spy. "Let's go. Wouldn't want to disappoint the lovely Helena."

Candy guided him through the music room, the library, the room with a full-scale and possibly functioning electric chair, the pool table room, the room with the pool, the room dominated by a huge aquarium, the den, and each bedroom. Gaudy and expensive artifacts from around the world competed for space, giving the house a constricted feel despite its enormity. A painting by a Ugandan artist stood out: Peaceful scene of the African brush that, on close inspection, revealed camouflaged leopard. The artist had merged brush and leopard almost seamlessly.

They explored the entire house except for one room off limits due to remodeling. Paul pretended indifference to the closed-off room but ten minutes later said he needed the bathroom. "My stomach's queasy. We're just about done, so go on downstairs and enjoy the rest of the party. I'll make sure Helena knows you're a wonderful docent."

Knowing nothing about picking locks, Paul found a pin in the medicine cabinet and prepared to learn. No need. One gentle twist, the doorknob turned, and the door swung open to an enormous room. It resembled an electronics warehouse with an extensive inventory that included microphones, computers, optical scanners, and other sophisticated-looking machinery, functions unknown. One entire wall featured a well-stocked gun rack. Venn's allegations no longer seemed far-fetched. Paul closed the door and went downstairs, stomach genuinely queasy.

The crowd thinned. Paul, mission accomplished, sought out Hal to say goodbye. Hal said, "Please stay so we can talk."

After ushering out the last guest but two, Hal took Paul's hand. "I trust you had a good time. Come, I'd like to introduce you to two dear friends. The Arabian charmer is Salim Alamdar," he said of a tall Arab in a gray business suit, "and this dashing bloke is Lucien Sartie." Lucien wore a hell's angels' tee shirt and had a long knife in a sheath clipped onto dirty jeans. Both men were in their late twenties and wore Patek Philippe watches—the only obvious commonalities between them. After handshakes all around, they made awkward small talk while Helena flounced around the room filling glasses. "Try this Joseph Drouhin Montrachet Marquis de Laguiche. It's extraordinary. Here, have some Egon Muller reisling. I got it for a steal—$360 a case." Paul suspected that Hal's mouthwash cost more than the merlot he'd brought.

Hal flicked a switch and the room filled with the sounds of Elton John. Pirouetting onto one of the six leather Italian sofas, and motioned his guests to each sit in another. "Tell me Paul, what do you think of my little pleasure palace?"

"Like your guests, fascinating."

"You're probably too polite to ask how I accumulated so much. Actually, this house is too small. I'm going to sell and relocate on ten acres in Laguna Beach."

"Now that you mention it, I've been trying to decide whether you look more like Jeff Bezos or Bill Gates."

Smiling, "You should see Salim's summer home in Spain. Maybe you will some day—or have your own."

Paul arched his eyebrows to convey approval of Spanish summer homes, and Hal continued. "After NYU I hired out as a statistical consultant. Made a decent salary, but the best part was getting into the books of major corporations. Then I met Salim. This sly dog persuaded me that my information might have substantial cash value. At a Chinese restaurant, he arranged for me to get a special fortune cookie: CASH PLUS INFORMATION YIELDS LOTS MORE CASH." Paul thought of the stupid messages he had failed to deliver.

Hal squeezed Salim's shoulders. "I asked Salim if he was courting me, and he gave an enthusiastic yes." Salim squirmed. "We've been partners ever since."

"And Lucien?"

"Lucien has access to a different type of sensitive information. Once Salim and I bonded, we advertised on computer bulletin boards for the exclusive services of a computer genius. We received more than 300 replies and flew several people out for interviews. Salim thought that Lucien outshone them all—and he's got the cutest buns I've ever seen. Lucien, stand up and show Paul your buns."

"Fuck you, fag."

"Computer whiz, great buns, and a beautiful way with words. Is it any wonder we made him a full partner!"

"You said I might own a summer home."

Salim winked. "For Arabs, friendship comes before business. Arabs take time getting to know potential colleagues, and they make friends for life. Americans are all business. They demand to know the bottom line. I like your attitude, Paul. I think I'm becoming American."

"Look, you've got money and Lucien's a computer whiz and Helena looks spectacular in a dress." Hal beamed. "But I've got nothing to contribute."

"Oh, dear boy, you're too modest. Your radio show is de rigueur among Berkeley's intelligentsia. I'll bet you can arrange interviews with anyone in the Bay Area. Nobel Prize winners from Berkeley and Stanford, computer entrepreneurs, military personnel at Lawrence Livermore laboratory. Anyone."

"So?"

Hal rubbed a finger across his neck, Lucien rolled his eyes. Hal said, "He's not obtuse, just naive. Have I mentioned that we met in an extraordinarily difficult class at NYU, and the big hunk outperformed me?" Turning toward Paul, "We need people at the forefront of knowledge. Once interviewed by you and charmed off their feet, they'll leap at the chance to attend an intimate gathering at your house. The three of us will provide the entertainment."

Hal seemed intent on proving he was a spy, though a pretty pathetic one. He lacked subtlety and spoke indiscreetly with someone he barely knew. Unless he killed people who turned him down. Lucien carried a knife, Salim's suit bulged ominously.

"Why do I get the impression that your 'entertainment' leads to felonies like industrial espionage and treason?"

Hal clapped, beaming at the others. "Told you he's a quick study."

Salim said, "My friend, the world's 500 richest people have combined assets equal to those of the bottom 2 1/2 billion. Their corporations rule the world. National boundaries are irrelevant. Large-scale wars cut into profits and treason doesn't pay."

"Too bad the CIA and federal courts don't agree."

Salim: "Their archaic views make buying and selling information the last great frontier."

"Lucrative and fun," Hal said, words accompanied by sly grin, "like peeking into a forbidden room. Of course, discretion is essential. Some forbidden rooms have hidden cameras."

Paul had underestimated badly. Struggling to maintain composure, he nevertheless realized that dissembling was futile. They knew. He watched Salim's hand slide to the bulge in his suit and Lucien move over to reach for his wine glass—innocuous perhaps, but placing him between Paul and the door.

"Assuming I say yes, what would my compensation be? Would I have a chance to become a partner?"

Hal clapped again. "I knew we could count on you. Excuse me for a few minutes. Salim will fill you in on the financial arrangement." Hal turned and ascended the staircase, heels clacking all the way up.

Lucien changed the music to loud, pulsating guitar. He unsheathed his wicked-looking knife and stroked it ostentatiously, eyes fixed unwaveringly on Paul. "So," he said mockingly, "I guess it's a sexual thing between you and Helena?" He strung out each syllable of "Helena."

"You've got the knife, so you get the girl. Helena is all yours."

"Touche," laughed Salim. "But I'm curious, why did you contact him?"

"I'm trying to put together a program with a panel of Easterners who've moved to the Bay Area."

"Have you set a date?"

The room was hot, the music pounding. Paul wiped a bead of sweat off his neck. "It's still up in the air."

"Maybe I can be a panelist. I'm from the Middle East."

Lucien said, "You must think we're loose cannons, telling you so much on the first date." He looked toward the door from which Hal had exited. "Let me assure you, we're pathologically careful and know more about you than your father—I mean your mother—your father died twelve years ago."

"Carelessness must be pretty serious in your line of work."

"We make very few mistakes—and always correct them promptly."

Paul wondered if Marv and Donna had been corrected mistakes. Salim answered his ringing cell phone. He spoke in Arabic, hung up, said, "I must go. I hope we'll meet again soon, Paul. Goodbye, Lucien. Say goodbye to Hal."

The door closed. Paul shifted uncomfortably in his chair. A minute passed. Paul opened the cabinet to the CD player. "Hope you don't mind, I'm going to turn the volume down a bit." Lucien didn't speak. He slid the flat part of the knife along his thigh, rotating it slowly and narrowing his eyes each time it pointed toward Paul. Then he abruptly stood up and, returning the knife to its sheath, walked to the door. "Maybe we'll meet again. Say goodbye to the fag."

Geezers, Day Two

They spent most of the first day watching videos, including some from Brent's early solitaire version. Then they reconvened shortly before dusk on the second day. Despite the cramped quarters the mood was festive, with the men generously applauding each others' creativity. They shouted gleefully or moaned in protest following each announced score. During frequent bathroom breaks, fueled by a limitless supply of aged scotch and rare wines, they discovered mutual interests and initiated business deals. For months afterwards, Wall Street felt reverberations.

The ex-CIA man said that Brent would have made a brilliant military tactician. A retired actor compared his directorial skills with those of Orson Welles. The men raised glasses in toast. Brent modestly said that they just needed a little experience to reach his level. He added, mysteriously, that they were in the midst of a work in progress. The men leaned forward anticipating an explanation, but his cell phone rang and he stopped in mid-sentence to answer. Grin spreading across his face, he said "Wonderful." Then, to his audience, "In five minutes I'd like you all to find seats and stop talking or making any other noise. If you have to use the bathroom, go now. I'm going to turn off the lights. Dominic will give each of you a mask. Put them on. They will be mildly inconvenient, but you'll understand in about fifteen minutes."

STILL AT HAL'S

PAUL SHOUTED "HAL, HELENA," but nobody answered. He picked up a *Cosmopolitan* and riffled through the pages, then rummaged around the kitchen for something to write on. He found a pen shaped like a penis, complete with dangling testicles, attached to a notepad. Its border looked like an open mouth. He scribbled a thank you and goodbye note and ran toward the door. Too slow. Just before he touched the door handle, the lights dimmed and electric guitars gave way to Johnny Mathis singing "Chances Are." Mathis' voice, activated by several tiny wall speakers, glided seductively around the room. A soft red spotlight moved synchronously with the music and directed Paul's eyes to the far corner. Music and spotlight ascended. Then slowly, tantalizingly, the ceiling opened.

Hal descended from a trapdoor in the room upstairs, bathed in soft light and gyrating coquettishly on a small platform. His tongue made slow circles around lipstick-painted, slightly parted mouth. He tossed Paul a yellow rose. Paul, rigid and unmoving, let it float to the floor inches away. Hal pirouetted off the platform, almost knocking over a lamp, and undulated toward Paul—cobra slithering toward petrified mouse. Paul retreated and fell into a sofa. Mathis sang "The Twelfth of Never."

Hal slid alongside Paul and murmured throatily, "Do you find me attractive?"

"Hal, I prefer women, and I'm in love with one."

"Helena," he corrected, not as easily deterred as Candy had been. His satin robe crept above the knee. Paul shuddered. Hal said, "Woody Allen said that bisexuality doubles your chances of getting a date. You should try it."

Paul stood up, "I've got to go."

"Wait, close your eyes, I want to show you something."

"Okay, but then I'm leaving." He covered his eyes. There was a soft rustling.

"Ta, ta," cooed Hal. "You can open now."

The robe lay on the ground next to Helena, who stood facing him with hands on hips, legs apart, swaying gently in time to the music. She wore a teddy nightie: pink, silk, and sheer, matching the one Marice had worn the night they'd first made love. They apparently patronized the same boutique. Helena's coy smile expressed the tacit assertion: Now you can appreciate my full beauty. Paul's lunch backed up into his throat. He said, "Goodbye, Hal."

Message

A message from Hal awaited on the answering machine: "There are dozens of radio people, and only one will become fabulously wealthy. I make the final choice, and my sofa is the casting couch. Please call."

OC

"Men are so simple and so much inclined to obey immediate needs that a deceiver will never lack victims for his deception." Machiavelli

In 1835, journalist Richard Locke wrote in the New York Sun that scientists had discovered an intelligent civilization of four-feet-tall, winged humanoid creatures on the moon. He quoted eminent astronomer Sir John Herschel's reports in the Edinburgh Journal of Science. The reports convinced thousands of readers.

William Albertson was a leading figure in the Communist Party. In 1964, his friends found a secret informant's report to the FBI in Albertson's handwriting, signed "Bill." He swore he hadn't written it, but the party expelled and ostracized him. He lost his job. Twelve years later, an internal FBI memorandum mistakenly made public detailed how the department's counterintelligence division had planted a fake report. In 1989, the U.S. government agreed to pay $170,000 to Albertson's widow.

Reprimand

Paul sought out Donna's mother at the service and gave her a watercolor of the view from his backyard. "Donna painted this, one of her many talents. Please take it. Also, the photograph. I made a copy." He had rehearsed a lie in case she asked when they'd last talked.

He had walked from BART to the church and began retracing his steps. Head bowed, shoulders slumped, he blamed Donna's death on his insufficient forcefulness. She'd still be alive if he'd demanded she meet him. The honk of a car interrupted his thoughts. Turning, he saw Venn. Everpresent cigar in mouth, head sticking out from the back seat of the limousine, his nemesis yelled "Get in. Tell me what happened."

"Give me a day or two. I just said goodbye to a dear friend."

"Rearrange your timetable. What happened?"

Paul glared into the limo but remained outside. Venn said, "I don't give a rat's fuck if you'd rather stand in the cold, but I want to know what happened." He retracted his head so Paul had to bend to be heard.

Paul gave what details he remembered. Venn nodded at the mention of Lucien and Salim, grimaced at the inadequate descriptions of the devices in the upstairs room, then bellowed when told how the night had ended. "You gutless piece of shit, did you think your assignment was just to get into his house? We've got to learn all his contacts and get him on tape making an illegal offer."

Paul said, "Screw you. I did what you told me."

"No, let Helena screw you."

"You knew about Hal!"

"Of course I knew. Now listen good. Nobody's asking you to fall on a grenade. You've just gotta spend one stinking night with a fag to help your country."

"Look, I agreed to cooperate, but I don't work for you. I am not a professional spy or spy-catcher, and I don't intend to change my sexual orientation."

"If something happens to honeypot, you won't have any sex. Don't blow your chance to save her and at the same time help your country."

Paul spotted two fellow mourners walking across the street and felt obliged to wave, but he hoped they wouldn't cross over. To his relief, they waved back and kept walking. Venn spread cheese on a cracker and offered it through the window. Paul pushed away his hand. He paused to take a deep breath. "Please explain why Marice is in danger. How is she involved?"

"Are you really this fucking stupid? Don't you understand by now that you're not supposed to ask questions? Now, what's it going to be?"

Barely audibly, "Whatever you say."

Venn said, "Good, it would be a pain in the ass to find someone who turns Helena on like you do." He rolled up the window. "Enjoy your walk." The limo roared off.

Bye Bye Baby

The ringing frightened Marice. She loved to hear Paul's voice, but speaking with him meant another round of dissembling. Her other main caller was Brent. If it was Brent… It was Brent. "Buenos dias. Do you want the good news first or the bad news?"

"I hope you rot in Hell."

Brent laughed. "You know, you religious folk have everything backwards. You think the Devil will punish me for my sins. Ha! He loves me, I make his life interesting. Your guy rewards the hypocrites, mine rewards sinners. I expect to be given a luxury pad in the choicest spot in Hell."

Not interested in a theological debate, she mumbled "Good news," certain that his cheerfulness signaled that the bad would be catastrophic.

"You have earned a roundtrip ticket to anywhere in the world. Just tell me the destination. You leave in two days and will be gone about two months."

"I couldn't leave my job just now even if I wanted to go."

"You'll find some excuse, and you'll receive more than double your salary while you're away. So, what'll it be? Paris, Amsterdam, Rio, name it."

"What is the bad news?"

"You must go alone and Joanna is the only one you can tell. You're an accomplished liar. Make up a good story for your boss and parents. Nothing at all for lover boy. Oh, and clean out your apartment. When you come back I'm going to move you to a nice pad in San Francisco."

Homounerotic

Paul had to arrange for his "Night of Great Unpleasantness" right on the heels of the funeral. He left home early, parked on the street, and opened a bottle of Jack Daniels. Tilting back his head, he swigged hoping for intoxication to the point of oblivion. The amber liquid burned his throat and he spit most out involuntarily, then had a fit of hiccupping. But he forced down enough to become tipsy. He stumbled down the driveway and rang the bell. Joel Grey sang his greeting.

Hal wore a black wig this time, same hair color as Marice's, cascading halfway to his waist. He smiled demurely, "Hi big boy."

"Listen Hal, I'm here because I want to be part of your group. But I don't want sex with you. Can't we be just friends and business partners?"

"Helena's the name." He twirled to display the long white dress from all sides. "Don't I look positively ravishing." Spinning closer, his hand brushed across Paul's crotch. Paul cringed, and Hal admonished, "Don't do that. It's not enough that we have unbridled, animal sex, you have to make me feel irresistible. Don't you think I am?"

"Hal, I don't find men sexually irresistible, but I can get you valuable information. Let's leave it at that?"

"Stop being so proletarian. Pretend you're a Sambian of New Guinea. Adolescent boys in that enlightened region are required to suck off older men over a period of years. It's a crucial step toward becoming a man." His hand found Paul's crotch again. "Dear boy, it's growing. I think you've just been playing hard to get. Now you're just hard."

Though sure his penis hadn't grown, the thought unnerved Paul. Dizzy from the whiskey, slightly nauseous, not able to think of anything else to do, he mechanically obeyed when Hal said, "Come, help me out of my dress." He remembered none of the ensuing details—until, a few weeks later, Brent mailed a videotape.

In the morning Hal kissed him goodbye and patted his butt. Paul ran to the car, desperate to get home to shower and try to scrub himself clean.

Parents

The week before Paul's college graduation, his father called to say he had been diagnosed with pancreatic cancer and given six months to live. Paul flew to Topeka, where his B.A. in philosophy got him a part-time job as a department store security guard. He spent nights with his parents. While his father still had strength, they attended a Royals' game and spent the last three innings arguing whether Brett had been a better all-around player than Bonds. Driving home, Paul marveled at how far away the horizon seemed. "In the Bay Area you can't see more than 100 feet beyond most freeways. This is like looking at a green ocean on a calm day."

The doctors administered drugs to relieve pain. They could do nothing to halt the cancer's spread, but their timetable was as accurate as a Dutch train schedule. The primary doctor advised that he be transferred to a hospital, but all three of the Charles Combes family refused. They wanted him comfortable in his own bed, not surrounded by stainless steel, whiteness, and the illusion of antiseptic conditions. Paul had read that doctors don't routinely clean their equipment after treating infectious patients, and as a result hospitals are a major source of disease transmission.

Charles Combes said he accepted impending death and regretted only that he wouldn't know grandchildren. He fought to stay awake while Paul described life in California and reminisced about childhood friends. When eyelids fluttered and chest momentarily stopped heaving, Paul stroked his forehead; but whenever Paul's narrative slowed, the feeble voice asked a question or made a comment to show he was still awake.

His mother listened with pet cockatiel on her shoulder, sometimes knitting, sometimes reminding them both of cute things little Paulie had done. She remembered the names of his teachers, his little injuries, all his big adventures. Charles Combes became comatose, and the doctor said that he could no longer see or hear and was oblivious to his surroundings. Paul continued to talk, massaged a limp hand, promised to take care of his mother, and told his father that he would miss him terribly. The breathing became labored, then shallower while Paul droned on. Just before the eyes closed for the last time, right after Paul and his mother said they loved him, they held hands and watched as two tears trickled down the sides of Charles Combes' face.

M & Ms

Paul relocated to the Bay Area and persuaded his mother to follow. She moved to Walnut Creek, a Bay Area suburb only a twenty minute car ride from Oakland. Shortly before Donna's death, Paul had invited her to dinner to meet Marice, and canceling would have provoked too many questions. He tossed a salad, put it in the refrigerator with two bottles of chardonnay, ordered a large pizza, and drove to Walnut Creek to pick her up.

Marice arrived holding an enormous bouquet of dianthus and lantana, bright flowers contrasting starkly with her dark mood. She harbored the terrible secret that Paul, so happy tonight, would be devastated tomorrow. She'd be gone without warning or explanation. She wondered if he'd still want her after two months. If Brent would ever allow her to explain.

While Audrey Combes scurried off to find a vase, Paul picked up his cell phone. "I want you two to stand together. This is a historic moment, the meeting of mom and Marice. My M & M girls." They put their arms around each other's waists, and Audrey scrutinized the face she suspected would be reflected in her grandchildren.

"Where did you buy such lovely flowers?"

"I stole them. My mom's a dedicated gardener and I take all her best work."

"Do you grow anything yourself?"

"My apartment doesn't have a backyard. I intend to have a big garden someday and grow lots of natives."

"You'll have to invite me, we Kansas people are fanatic about gardens. My apartment is tiny, but I grow basil and pineapple sage. Would you like cuttings?"

"I cook with basil all the time, and love the smell of pineapple sage. Will you deliver the cuttings and stay for a home-cooked Mexican dinner?"

Alone in the kitchen, Paul uncorked the wine. Images of Marvin, Donna, and Hal intruded on all his happy thoughts, and he knew he'd need time to heal. Still, it comforted him that the M & Ms had developed an instant rapport.

Audrey patted a sofa cushion, inviting Marice to sit next to her. "I brought a photo album. Thought you might want to see pictures of Paul at different ages."

Colombo jumped on top of the album, and Marice resettled him on her lap. That suited Colombo just fine.

Paul groaned, "I expected some intelligent conversation. Now I'll just have to listen to you two marveling about how cute I was."

Audrey flipped open the album to a second grade group photo. She pointed to little Paul and noted that he was already reading at the fifth grade level. Marice traced her finger around the tiny image, then sadly shook her head. "He wasn't at all cute. Actually, rather ugly."

Paul interrupted his pouring to turn. He didn't see the grin. Audrey swallowed a protest, covered her mouth, and tittered. Marice turned to a new page. "Ugliest kid I ever saw." Audrey poked her in the ribs.

Paul handed them each a wine glass. "The girls didn't think I was ugly. Mom, show her those steamy pictures of me and Brenda. That'll put her in her place."

By the time they reached a photo of three-year-olds Paul and Brenda, naked, splashing gleefully in a wading pool, the first wine bottle stood empty and Audrey and Marice had their arms draped around each other. The next page revealed the two toddlers kissing. Audrey patted Marice's hand and said, "Don't worry dear, she was just a bimbo." They greeted each new picture with increasing decibels of laughter. Still several pages from the end, Audrey jumped up and ran to the bathroom. She emerged holding her chest and said, "I almost peed in my pants." Paul hadn't seen her so lighthearted in years.

When they dropped Audrey off at her condo several hours later, the women hugged like mother and daughter. Audrey said, "Paul's father would have been very happy."

Marice's head dropped onto his chest for the ride home, and he drove one-handed, right arm wrapped around her shoulders. She said, "Your mom is wonderful."

Paul agreed. "I think you two are going to be good friends." She forced a smile, stifling a scream, knowing that this would be their last time together for at least two months. She rubbed her hand across his knee. He stopped at a traffic light and leaned over to kiss her forehead. She raised her head, and the kiss changed from tender to passionate. She promised herself to give him the most memorable night of his life.

Marice pulled him up the stairs and onto the bed, then fluffed up a pillow and tucked it behind his neck. Men had gawked at her since she'd turned twelve, and she'd always hated it. Tonight was different. Tonight she intended to provoke gawking. For phase one. Positioning herself two steps back from the bed, legs slightly apart, she undid the top button of her blouse. Slowly, very slowly, the next one. Feeling more awkward than erotic, she suppressed a giggle. His gaping mouth and dilated pupils convinced her to continue. She thrust out her chest and undid another button. Only one left.

Paul raised himself on his elbows. "You're blushing."

"I'm sorry Paul, this feels weird. Just give me a few seconds."

"Honey, come to bed and lie next to me."

Still dumbfounded by her eagerness to please him, overwhelmed by her beauty and sensuousness, he wanted nothing so much as to please her in return. But he couldn't get sexually aroused. The previous twenty-four hours had left too much pain.

Dinner had been postscript to Donna's funeral and the night with Hal, and their images still floated in his head. Waves of sorrow washed over him, and his penis remained unerect. "Honey, I want to hold you next to me all night, but I can't make love tonight. I'm sorry. Tomorrow will be better."

Knowing that tomorrow would be infinitely worse, Marice pressed tightly against him. "Silly, it's alright. We are making love."

In the morning, Paul showered and shaved while she fixed blueberry pancakes, orange juice, and coffee. Carefully following instructions, she scribbled two notes, left one under the coffee mug, and pocketed the other for delivery to Brent. She took nothing else with her.

Paul emerged from the bathroom determined to start putting his life in order, a difficult process that he expected would be eased by his new and wonderful ally. Smelling the fresh brewed coffee sent a caffeine jolt to his brain, and he patted his stomach appreciatively at the rest of the beautifully prepared breakfast. Assuming that Marice had walked to the store for an additional treat, he covered the food to keep it hot while awaiting her return. The coffee aroma proving irresistible, he lifted the mug.

"I'm crazy in love & love a crazy. Bye for now."

He hadn't heard the phone while showering and now noticed the blinking answering machine. It played back a brief message from Hal. "I hope you enjoyed last night as much as I did, but a long-term relationship would be impractical. Au revoir, sweetie."

Hal had rejected him. Rejection that under other circumstances might have caused a bitter laugh, at present unnerved. No longer of use to Venn, he might end up on a hit list. Screaming "Son of a bitch" at the top of his lungs didn't improve matters, so he smashed his fist against a wall. The impact dislodged a small painting, which clattered to the floor startling Colombo and sending the terrified cat scurrying. Hand throbbing, he dialed Marice and left a message, "You might be in danger. Get out of town immediately. Don't call me or come back till you see a classified ad in the *Trib* addressed to your pretend-wrestling name.

I'll use the name of the guy who gave us Belafonte tickets. Sorry to be so mysterious. Be careful. I love you."

While soaking the hand in Epsom salts and waiting for Venn to re-establish contact, Paul phoned Arlene, the station manager. He said he needed two weeks off "to deal with a crisis." His right index finger had swollen and become discolored. He fidgeted for an hour, then drove to Kaiser Hospital and told the intake nurse he'd hurt the finger playing basketball. X-rays confirmed a break, and an intern splinted the finger. He rushed home but had no messages.

Nobody answered the bell. Hoping she'd followed the phone directions, he nevertheless repeated them on a scrap of paper and slipped it under her door. He drove to the College Avenue address written on the first undelivered package. A coffee shop. Feeling foolish, he asked the cashier if she'd ever heard the name Marvin Flynn. She shook her head. Donna Brookens? Venn? No, no. Handing her twenty dollars and a paper with his name and phone number, he asked her to check with the other workers and regular customers and get back to him if anything turned up. The second address, an apartment complex on Grand, took much longer to go through but with the same negative results.

His next stop was the Department of Motor Vehicles to tell about being sideswiped by a driver in a black Mercedes who had sped off. He'd written down the license number and needed a corresponding address. He offered the paper on which he'd scribbled Venn's number. The clerk handed him a form to be signed, notarized, and mailed to Sacramento. Paul pleaded fruitlessly for a few minutes, then thought of an alternative. He called Leonard, whose vast network of friends included a Hertz data processor and a VISA executive. Soon he had an address on Pacific Heights in San Francisco. Leonard insisted on tagging along.

OC

The human being is a blind man who dreams that he can see. Friedrich Hebbel.

Man is what he believes. Chekkov.

Baby elephants in India are tied to a wooden pole that they try to but cannot break. Soon, conditioned into believing they can't break it, they stop trying. Thus, mature, powerful elephants remain shackled to small, easily breakable poles.

Nathan Sharfman studied at Harvard with brilliant philosopher Alfred North Whitehead, who proclaimed Sharfman the hope of American philosophy. The hope finished his professional career as a taxicab driver.

Breaking and Entering

They reached the huge Victorian, on the corner of two quiet streets, just before dark. Nobody answered the bell, so Paul plopped down on the front steps determined to wait for somebody to arrive. Leonard was less patient. He yanked at the doorknob and shouted "Hello, anyone home?" Although the doorknob didn't budge, the shouting prompted the opening of two windows in neighboring houses. Leonard shrugged and motioned Paul to follow him back to the car. "Let's park on a side street. We can sneak back and jimmy a side window."

"You're crazy. That's breaking and entering."

"Don't worry homeboy. Niggers got great breakin' and enterin' genes. Ain't you read *The Bell Curve*?"

The delicate flowers of a large jacaranda tree had fallen in the backyard area and covered it like a carpet of blue snowflakes. They found a ground floor window slightly ajar. Leonard wriggled a screwdriver to pry it open, then forced his fingers underneath and lifted. Although the splint handicapped him, Paul managed to crawl through behind Leonard into a mammoth, bare living room. A strong smell of disinfectant suggested that the place had recently been vacated and cleaned.

"What if there's a dog?"

"Niggers got great runnin' genes too."

"Quit messing around. I'm scared."

"You're right, I'm scared too. I'll talk caucasian."

"Looks like nobody lives here. Your friend must have given you the wrong address."

"Maybe, but we're dirty and already broke the law, so let's look around." He flicked a switch. Nothing happened. They investigated a squeak from one of the downstairs bedrooms. Nothing. Leonard said, "Probably a rat. Empty houses magnify sounds." He climbed the stairs to poke around on the second floor, leaving Paul to check the kitchen. Seconds later Leonard shouted, "Get your ass up here. We've found the Mint."

Paul raced upstairs to see Leonard, beaming, pointing to a small desk on which sat a telephone and a three-inch high stack of $100 bills. Some bills had slipped through his fingers and littered the floor, while a few floated toward Paul like confetti. "They were just lying here waiting."

A slip of paper under the stack had escaped Leonard's notice. While he counted the money, Paul picked it up. He read:

Mr. Combes: Dont try 2 find me. It woud b hazardous & u woud hav no recours 4 further damages. Dont feel harsh towrd Hal. He knows no mor than u. I hope the money makes the decepton (which ws necesry) bearabl.

Lt. Col. Venn

The deception, whatever the explanation, might have been bearable except for two additional sentences.

Im sorry P. U wil always b specil. M.

His moan erupted so loudly and unexpectedly that Leonard dropped everything. Leaving the bills scattered, he gently extracted the paper from Paul's trembling hand.

Paul collapsed into a sitting position against the wall, nauseous and with a dull ache in his chest. Leonard squatted alongside. "I'm so sorry Paul. I know how much she meant." Paul patted Leonard's hand but wished his friend would disappear. Leonard inhibited him from screaming.

The flashlight flickered and the room grew dark. Leonard said they should leave before anyone came. Paul told him to take the money and go. "You're my best friend and you earned it." Voice choking, "They led me here. Whoever they are, whatever their reason, they played me like a fish."

"We'll discuss the money later. I'm not leaving without you, so if I get busted it'll be on your conscience." Paul's feeble smile conveyed the message that smiling took effort.

Leonard said, "I never told you about my big love, shortly before we met. Andrea was only nineteen, I was twenty-nine. But she was the mature, sophisticated one. I asked her to marry me but she said no. Too young. Besides, her blackass family hated me. They didn't trust a black man with green eyes. Talk about racism. I pushed hard, and eventually she told me she didn't want to see me any more. I found out that she married some law student six months later. I still think about her."

Despite the warm summer night, Paul started shivering. He said, "My parents were high school sweethearts and stayed married for forty years. I wanted to be like them, to fall in love just once."

Leonard pounded fist into hand. "We can find Venn. We'll make that bastard pay."

Paul didn't care. He had lost Marice. He had never had Marice. His pain was terrible and infinite.

Leonard said, "I'm going downstairs." Nodding took all Paul's strength—a battery-powered mechanism with a dead battery.

Leonard punched the phone's automatic redial. "Hello, this is Bob Lowery from radio station KFRC. Your number has been picked at random from the telephone directory. If you guess the paid attendance at today's Giants game and get within 5,000, you'll get fifty cents for each person there."

The ear at the other end said "Screw you" and hung up. No name, no address. Leonard climbed back upstairs and whispered that he had to find a store. Paul remained inert and still hadn't moved when Leonard returned thirty minutes later with a tape recorder. Leonard repunched automatic redial and recorded the dialing sounds. "My friend at the phone company can listen to the sounds and figure out the number. Then he'll come up with an address." Paul didn't much care. But he finally acquiesced when Leonard insisted that they leave the house.

Leonard led Paul upstairs to the spare bedroom in his house. He made chamomile tea, and they talked until Paul said he thought he could sleep. Leonard arose twice during the night to check on him. His friend slept noisily and fitfully but remained in bed, didn't go off doing something rash. In the morning, Leonard's friend at the phone company said the tape recorder had been unnecessary. Given the Pacific Heights address, the friend provided a print-out of all the phone numbers, addresses attached, that had been called from that telephone during the past month.

B & E: Part II

The closest address, on Cedar Street in Berkeley, was about a mile from Paul's house and had been called recently and the most often. Paul said he would start the investigation there and insisted on going alone. "I shouldn't have let you go to that other place. You were fantastic and I love you, but this is my problem, not yours. Besides, if something happens, I need you to tell the police." They hugged goodbye.

He parked shortly before dusk and exited the Prius wearing dark clothes, running shoes, and a Giants cap with the visor pulled low across his forehead. Poor sleep plus general malaise had left him considerably sub par, but anger and fear combined to clear his head. Pedestrian traffic was light on the quiet street, and nobody lingered. He walked casually past the small, undistinguished A-frame with drawn blinds. The dark interior convinced him that nobody was home. He crossed the street and walked back, started to knock, then decided to wait for total darkness. He drove to a Lucky store and bought laundry detergent and pretzels, all the while regretting that he didn't have Leonard alongside making wisecracks. Night fell, yet the house remained dark. He rang the bell, reasonably certain that nobody would answer and having no plan if someone did. He tugged at the doorknob. It didn't budge, so he returned to the car for a flashlight and crowbar, intending for the second time in two days to break into a house. He stuffed the tools into a shopping bag.

Paul brushed burning droplets of sweat from his eyes and flicked at a mosquito buzzing his ear. He noticed a man looking out an upstairs window in a house across the street, so walked to the corner and back. The man was no longer there, so he had no more excuses to delay. He opened a gate at the side of the house and scampered to the back, ducking under a large densely foliated tree that hid him securely while he planned his next move. He hefted the crowbar—his only weapon should the need arise, but he doubted that he'd have the guts to use it.

A branch creaked. Twenty feet overhead, a squirrel completed an acrobatic leap. Squirrels! He hated them.

He saw a small folding chair leaning against a young oak—a providential burglary accessory. He positioned it under a nearby window, stood on the chair, and slid the window high enough so that he could crawl through. The splint still hampered him. Standing on his toes, he peeked into the room and saw nothing out of the ordinary. He hesitated. Not too late to turn back. No, he was determined to learn who had wrecked his life and why. Hoisting himself, he wriggled through and landed on a wobbly dresser. His weight tilted the dresser just enough to dislodge a cup perched on the edge, which shattered noisily on the hardwood floor. Though sure the house was empty, he froze for several seconds, white-knuckled hands squeezing flashlight and crowbar, heart pounding furiously.

He held his breath while the crashing noises reverberated, exhaled only when they had completely died. Nobody burst into the room, no alarm bell rang. The absence of response gave him courage to ease down from the dresser. He began a systematic rummaging, at all times alert for the sound of a key in the front door. The dresser drawers contained nothing unusual: just neatly folded socks, tee shirts, and boxer shorts. A wall shelf held several paperbacks. Two men's suits and several shirts and pants hung in a closet. This house, unlike the Victorian, was clearly lived in—and given the limited information that had drawn him here, probably by a respectable person. Even liberal Berkeley has an NRA chapter with members eager to test their weapons on craven burglars. Although he doubted he'd find anything useful, and mindful that each moment increased his chance of being discovered, he proceeded slowly because he had no idea what to look for. He put his ear to the door. Hearing nothing, he took a deep breath and prepared to expand the search. Flashlight in damaged right hand, crowbar in left, he pushed the door open into the living room.

And was greeted by the glare of a spotlight. Momentarily blinded, he raised his hands to shield his eyes and struck the flashlight against his forehead. A voice boomed out like that of a public address announcer at a boxing match: "Gentlemen, let's give a big hand to Paul Combes, cat burglar extraordinaire." The spotlight swept the living room to reveal a group of masked men, clapping, stamping their feet, and shouting "Bravo" and "Well done." Paul retreated into the bedroom. The PA announcer called out "Hey dickhead, don't run away. Come give your fans a glimpse."

The announcer raised his hands triumphantly, patiently waiting for the commotion to diminish. "Gentlemen, I hope that the touching saga of Mr. Combes will inspire you to even greater heights of creativity. Now, if you don't mind, I'd like to debrief him in private. Thank you for indulging me."

A voice called out, "Let's hear a few words from Mr. Combes." Laughter, then a shout, "Speech, Mr. Combes, speech." Others joined in the call. Paul inched into the doorway, crowbar gripped tightly in his good hand. Brent shook his head. "Mr. Combes would not be a good speaker today." He pointed, and Dominic rushed to hold open the front door. The men filed out onto the quiet street of the middle class Berkeley neighborhood, each soon met by a chauffeured limousine.

Paul watched them leave. Once alone with Brent and Dominic, he said, "Whoever you are and whatever this is about, if you're responsible for what's happened to me in the last few days, I'm going to hurt you."

"Better take a close look at my boy here. Dominic used to fight as a light heavy—no speed, no grace, but a head like a rock. Dom, show him, put a hole in that wall." Dominic hesitated, and Brent said "Go ahead boy, now." Dominic lowered his head and butted the wall, creating a small fissure in the wall and a smaller one on his head. "C'mere Dom." Brent kissed the top of the reddening head and pointed to the door. "Go put something on that cut and then take a break outside." Turning to Paul, "I'm a pretty tough old geezer myself. Besides,—" He withdrew a gun from his jacket and put it on a coffee table—"I've got this, and you're in no condition to fight. That finger looks broken."

Brent walked to the kitchen and returned with two glasses and a pitcher of beer. Paul glowered. His host took a long swig, nodded appreciatively, then belched and wiped a hand slowly across his mouth.

"Let me give you a brief autobiography as I learned it from my drunken Aunt Millie. My old man wanted my mother to see an abortion doctor, and that started a never-ending fight. He got booted from the hospital about the time her water broke. So he went to a bar and started brawling. Nobody knows the whole story, but he died in police custody. An ambulance chaser reached my mother, said there were rumors of police brutality, and convinced her to sue for wrongful death. What a fucking joke. Aunt Millie swears the old lady hated him and it was the most rightful death ever. But the jury saw a grieving widow with a newborn baby and awarded her a $500,000 settlement. People get that today for losing a toenail, but it was big money back then. She fell for a seedy insurance salesman who convinced her to buy a humongous policy and, wouldn't you know, they were both killed in a car wreck a year later. So the suits set up a trust fund, the money grew, and on my twenty-first birthday I joined the upper crust."

"Great story, maybe a bit oversentimental, but what does any of that have to do with me?"

"It's unfair that I have so much more money than you but have to watch the same TV programs, listen to the same music, breathe the same fucking air. In medieval times, peasants could never leave their villages and had to always wear black or brown.

Today, college students go on safaris, the Salvation Army sells designer clothes, and if some dumb slob wants to blow a week's salary he can pig out at Chez Panisse."

"So, how did you correct those injustices? How do you use your billions?"

"Barely over a billion. I'm not even on Forbe's list. Of course, most of my assets are hidden."

"That doesn't answer the question?"

"I saw an incredible movie, *The Tenth Victim*, about the sport of the future. Every contestant tries to kill everybody else and the last one standing wins. What made it special is that people were prey, which gave me an idea for a game where money would mean something. Killing is boring, nothing like getting people to do crazy things. So I started a game for the filthy rich. We pick targets and compete to get them to self-destruct. But we get them to do it with style. It'll blow you away when you learn how easily people can be persuaded that their best friend is cheating them, their wife is fucking the hairdresser, even that they've seen a flying saucer or talked to God. It requires creativity, which is why I got you involved."

"You said no killing. What happened to Marvin Flynn and Donna Brookens?"

"I said that killing is boring. I don't mind if it's done with panache. Or if the victims are what military people call 'collateral damage.' Besides, don't you liberals always argue that the world's overpopulated."

"How did Marice fit in?"

"Every player rounds up a bunch of people and pays them to act. If they're good enough they can work full-time and earn a decent living. Your slut fit in beautifully, though I worried that you'd realize a babe like her wouldn't normally give someone like you the time of day." Moving his hand to his crotch, "Unless, of course, you were rich like me."

Paul stared impotently. Brent kept pounding away.

"Some of my troupe are pros. Venn's a high-ranking retired

Marine officer and Steige was a real police captain. They both have friends in high places and can call in all sorts of favors. We assumed you'd go to the police and arranged the set-up on short notice. Hal's an amateur. You think that stupid fucker could have gotten such a house on his own! He's not a transvestite and his *Cage Aux Folles* impersonation probably went over the top, but he had a great time and says you were fabulous. My video tapes of Hal with his mouth around your dick, and you bawling on the floor after reading slut's note—I'll probably watch those every Christmas."

That was the straw that broke... Screaming, "You bastard, you won't have another Christmas," Paul flung the crowbar. It sailed over Brent's head, close enough to startle him into dropping the gun. Paul charged, knowing he had just moments. A hook with his good left hand rocked Brent's temple, and the older man's hands lifted to shield his head. That exposed the ample gut, and Paul followed with an uppercut. Brent's hands dropped, opening the face for a smashing hook to the eye. Brent sagged to the floor.

Dominic burst in. Paul crouched in a boxer's stance but never had a chance. A powerful left/right combination landed flush on his chest and nose, buckling his knees. Dominic cocked his arm again ready to inflict serious damage, but Brent called out, "Stop. Help me up." Dominic kicked Paul's legs from under him before tugging Brent from the floor. Brent's smile returned, and he said, "You got off on hitting me, didn't you. Revenge is a great high. Some guy once shafted me in a business deal, and a bitch once refused to talk to me in a singles bar. They're both a lot uglier now. Magic moments."

Dazed, sore hand pressing against bleeding nose, Paul rose unsteadily from the floor. He expected to be made instantly uglier. Brent said, "Let him go. He'd do us no good damaged." To Paul, "I'll pretend we're even. But if you ever do anything so stupid again, you're a dead man." With exaggerated politeness, "Maybe now you're ready for a drink. It's time I explained why I brought you here."

Paul accepted a glass of water. With Dominic standing

menacingly nearby, any additional acts of bravado would have ended badly. Despite his unhappy prospects, he observed with satisfaction that a welt had formed under Brent's eye.

"You said you brought me here. What if I hadn't gone to the supermarket where I met her?" ('her'—he couldn't bring himself to utter the name). "What if I hadn't memorized Venn's license number or tracked you here?"

"You think that memorizing the license plate was a stroke of brilliance? Truth is, you're a dumb shit. You missed so many clues, I thought of painting an arrow from your house to here. Oh, by the way, don't call the Yankees for a tryout. My pitcher worked hard at throwing the ball where you could hit it."

After hearing about Marice, the softball news had no impact. Dead men don't feel pain. Paul said, "I still don't understand."

"Instead of poker parties, me and my friends pick competing goals for each target, like having them run onstage naked during a symphony recital or crawl through the bedroom window of a house in search of a lost love. We draw lots to see who gets which goal, then race to get the target to ours first."

"The only part I don't believe is that you've got friends."

Brent clapped. "His rapier wit returns. Good, but wrong. Money buys everything, even friends. Incidentally, like all good citizens, we reward diversity. That's why my boys insulted your nigger friend. Leonard got me a nice affirmative action bonus. You had balls to butt into that fight, but it was pretty stupid. If they weren't following a script they might have killed you. I don't hire losers."

Paul rubbed his hand across the scar. "You provoked that fight to manipulate me? Is that when I became your target?"

Brent winked. "Let's just say that dear mom and dad were really yours. Beyond that…" His voice trailed off until only a smirk remained. Resuming the narrative, "My former script writer noticed that you like inspirational sayings like that dumb one in the room where you work out. That's why we had you deliver packages with sayings."

"What happened to your former script writer?"

"He didn't work out. But before he departed, he helped out with many of last year's human interest stories. Remember the $400,000 a year CEO who resigned to join a kibbutz, or the television preacher who admitted having sex with an underage girl?"

Paul kept his face expressionless to deny Brent the satisfaction of seeing his pain—but his stomach churned while he tried to comprehend the implications of what had just been said. Would Paul have to reinterpret his life? He conjured up memories from his first week in Oakland. Incidents at NYU, KU. Grade school. Brent had hinted that he'd instigated some of those events. That he had orchestrated some—maybe most—of the significant and trivial aspects of Paul's entire life. Paul forced himself to focus on the present. Recalling his elation at hearing news of the arrest and prosecution of the smarmy, self-righteous TV preacher, he mumbled, "You had something to do with the Shipley case?"

Brent picked his nose and flicked a booger to the floor. He snapped his fingers, and Dominic went into the second bedroom, emerging a moment later holding a small sheath of papers. He handed the sheath to Paul. Brent said, "Read our rule book."

Paul flung the sheaf to the floor. "The hell with you. I'm trying to decide whether to have you arrested for assault or murder."

"Remember three things. First, you broke into my house. Second, you have no evidence of my involvement in anything illegal. The police would laugh at you. Oh, I forgot, they already did. Third, and most important, I'm in charge. I brought you here so you could work for me. Some of the stories you've written show potential. We can't be satisfied just getting targets to their goals, we've got to figure out how to get them there in style. That'll be your job, like writing movie scripts. I'll see that the scripts are carried out. I'm a great director."

"Fuck you."

"Didja know, psychiatric residents at Langley Porter Institute in San Fran used to take LSD and other drugs as part of their training. The idea was, they had to experience being mentally ill in order to treat mental illness. My training is just as rigorous. Before I add anyone to my writing stable, he has to know what it feels like to get worked over by a writer."

"You're sick."

"Use up your clichés now. When you're on the payroll they won't be tolerated. Here's why you're gonna work for me. First, you'll get rich. Second, you'll find out if you have the imagination and creativity to make it as a serious writer. Best of all, you'll realize that you can completely change another person's universe. Maybe that doesn't seem like much right now, but someday it'll make you come."

Paul slumped in his chair, tired, angry, and afraid. He said softly, "No thanks, I'm satisfied with God's universe; I don't want to make changes."

"You're pathetic," snarled Brent. "I change his universe every day."

"Maybe I can't stop you from playing God, but I won't help."

"Why don't people mind when God plays God but get upset when anyone else does? Why does your bible lavish praise on a sadist who tormented Job and forced Abraham to consent to kill his own son."

Dominic retrieved the sheaf and thrust it into Paul's hand. Brent said, "Oh, incidentally, some of the players think the game would be more challenging if we made targets aware of their status. You could be our pioneer."

He took back the sheath for a moment. "Read this. If you don't think our game is more fun than Scrabble and group sex, use it as evidence." He scribbled a phone number on the top sheet. "Call me." To Dominic, "Dickhead's ready to go. Escort him to his car."

A neighbor's trash can sat curbside about fifty feet away. Paul double parked, honked to get attention, and with exaggerated movements threw the papers inside and drove off. Two hundred yards further, he turned back. Brent had been right, the sheaf could be used as evidence. He reached inside the wastebasket and retrieved it, now wet and sticky from contact with unknown substances. Looking back toward the A-frame, he saw Brent watching from the window, waving and grinning. He drove a few blocks further, parked on a quiet street, and separated the dripping papers. Of heavy parchment and engraved with gold lettering, they bore the title: ONTOLOGICAL CONFIGURATIONS.

Back to Kaiser

Kaiser's emergency room intake worker scanned Paul's medical record. "Gee, you're having a run of bad luck. Broken finger last week, now your nose. Looks broke to me."

Paranoiagenesis

Freud wrote that depression is anger turned inward. Paul's anger radiated outward, alternately and in roughly equal parts toward Brent and Marice. But depressed he was. His normally hearty appetite began to resemble that of a chemotherapy patient. Tortured sleep inevitably featured Marice. In some nightmares she cackled while monsters devoured him, in others she copulated lustily with several men while he watched helplessly. He called, but her phone had been disconnected. People at La Raza swore they knew no way to contact her. Nobody answered her doorbell, and though he drove by the building daily she never appeared.

He read and reread Ontological Configurations, each time thinking wistfully that his dad would have given wise counsel. He announced to Leonard's answering machine that he needed a few days of solitude. Resuming his spot at the station, he feigned cheerfulness and conducted a series of interviews that, though passable, lacked humor and were devoid of insightful comments. He avoided co-workers whenever possible.

Arlene tried drawing him out about his obvious unhappiness. Failing that, she arranged for a distinguished psychiatrist to appear as a guest on his show. Dr. Donald Peters described the classic symptoms of depression: loss of appetite, insomnia, and reduced sex drive. He cited studies showing that treatment works, yet more than two-thirds of severe depressives in the U.S. never receive any. After the show, Peters said that car trouble had forced him to take a taxi to the station. He asked if Paul could drive him to BART. When he mentioned his home address, Paul realized that they were almost neighbors (no accident) and offered to drive him straight home. They talked, and Paul said that his life had been good until a recent terrible sequence of events. Since then, he'd experienced all the symptoms Dr. Peters had mentioned. The psychiatrist urged him to get help and offered his own services. Paul said he'd like to start immediately.

The sessions were fruitless. He never mentioned Marice, Venn, or Brent, never Marvin or Donna. After the fourth meeting, the psychiatrist stated the obvious: "We're not progressing." Paul agreed to try an antidepressant drug, and Peters scribbled a prescription for Paxil.

Determined to figure out a way to stop Brent, though unsure whether his primary motive was to prevent others from being hurt or simple revenge, Paul invited Leonard and Cody Certner to dinner. Though he didn't know the singer very well, they'd shared some laughs. Leonard arrived first and saw his friend, three-day stubble covering his face, smelling badly, and ten pounds lighter than when they'd last gotten together. "Man, you look like shit. What's going on?"

"I want you to read something." Paul handed him "Ontological Configurations" and an Anchor Steam beer. While Leonard read, Paul riffled through his tiny photo album for the dozenth time that night. There was Marice, there were Marice and his mother, there were Marice and Colombo, there was Marice ...

Leonard cleared his throat. "I'm glad you're writing again. It'll help you get over that woman. This is an interesting premise. Not real plausible, but you can probably fix it."

"I didn't write that."

Paul explained about the Cedar Street house and Brent and the game. Leonard's head slumped into his hands, and he whispered, "Those boys must be stopped. They could do serious damage."

"They've already done serious damage, including at least two murders."

A loud knock announced Cody's arrival. He strutted into the room wearing a psychedelic shirt, tight black pants, and two gold necklaces. "Can't stay too long. There's a pair of twins built like you wouldn't believe who are dying to meet me. They promised to do whatever I want." He punctuated his remarks by sticking out his tongue and panting. Paul, wincing, introduced the two men. Cody said, "Only time I ever seen black people with green eyes was in Louisiana. That where you from?" Leonard nodded, and Paul filled him in on the recent events. Cody's head swung sharply from side to side, the long blond mane whipping around his eyes. Suddenly brightening, he said, "Listen, we're going on a month-long east coast tour in August. How about coming along? You can be our publicist."

"That wouldn't solve anything."

Cody disagreed. "Great looking chicks rush on stage after every show. They want to meet and please anyone associated with the band. I guarantee, someone will make you forget what's-her-name. Leonard, you're invited too. Can you drive a bus?"

Paul said, "Thanks, but first let's figure out how to stop those people."

Leonard handed Cody the folder. "Why don't you read this. There aren't any sex scenes but it's short with only a few big words." Sarcasm unnoticed, Cody popped open a beer, flopped on the chair, and started reading. Moments later he whistled and slapped his thigh approvingly, apparently recognizing the game as a pathway that could launch him to new creative heights. Paul motioned Leonard to the kitchen. "Bad mistake inviting Cody. I thought I knew him, but he's ready to join the league or start his own."

Leonard shrugged, "You've been hanging out with some electrifying people: Cody, Brent, Dominic, Hal, Venn. I'm honored to be your friend."

Paul punched his arm and both laughed weakly. "Should we tell him he'd better hurry and hook up with those twins? Maybe he'd just forget the whole night."

"We should get him drunk and tell him he dreamed the whole thing."

An angry scream from the next room cut short their discussion. Cody rushed out an instant later, tossing the folder across the room. "I'm out of here." Fighting off Paul's restraining hand, he whimpered, "You stupid bastards, stay away from me."

"What's wrong?"

"Didn't you read about the secrecy committee? I'm in deep shit."

Paul asked, "What are you talking about? Nobody knows I've told you anything."

"Right," he sneered, rushing past Paul to the door, "they spend ten million dollars for secrecy and then hand out the rules like *Watchtower* and *Awake*."

"Wait, Cody."

He jumped in the car and shouted, "Don't call me."

Leonard said "Let him go." Then, decisively, "Let's get out of here. My car. Yours probably has a bug."

"Are you going paranoid on me too?"

"Your singer friend thinks differently from us. Good you invited him, 'cause we needed that thinking. He was right, those guys take their game seriously, and they can afford the equipment to track your movements."

Leonard parked two blocks from Telegraph Avenue, and they walked to the bustling street. On warm nights, Telegraph attracts more diverse peoples than almost any area of comparable size in the world. Whites, Blacks, Mexicans, Native Americans, Japanese, Chinese, Iranians, Indians, Vietnamese, and Cambodians all intermingle. Groups of college kids browse in Moe's bookstore, aged hippies look in headshops and poster stores, and computer whizzes and would-be poets talk over cappucinos in Cafe Med. Panhandlers wait outside, and teenagers with spiked blue and pink hair rollerskate in the street. Policemen with beards dismount periodically from their bikes to engage passersby in friendly conversations. Paul thought ruefully that Telegraph was a gold mine for Brent.

Leonard said the money they'd found had totaled more than $4,000. He ordered burritos for both of them, and they found an unoccupied bench outside. A flautist sat cross-legged a few feet away, playing for donations. Leonard deposited several coins in her basket, then rubbed his chin vigorously as he always did when nervous. He chewed slowly, wiped his face, and at last broke their silence.

"You won't like my advice."

"Won't know till I hear. But I sure don't like my present situation."

"Could you kill a bad person to save a good person's life?"

Paul glowered at his friend.

"Answer me, could you?"

"Leonard, no ridiculous hypotheticals. This is too serious. Do you have advice that doesn't involve my becoming a murderer?"

Paul's animated and overly loud response caused the flautist to stop momentarily. She stared at the two men, wondering if she should find a more congenial spot.

"Just answer."

"Maybe under some circumstances I could kill somebody, but I don't want to find out."

"For me there's no doubt. If my mom's life was threatened, or Konesha's, or even a useless person like you, I could kill."

"Thanks, I'll sleep better tonight, but I'm not going to kill Brent."

"You could hire somebody."

"Same difference."

"He murdered two people you knew, one of them a good friend. Maybe I'm next. Maybe your mother."

"I don't know for sure that he killed anyone."

"Yeah, whatever. But think about it, sometimes the only way to be moral is to do what most people would call immoral."

"What's Plan B?"

"Tell Brent you'll write for him."

By broaching the unthinkable, Leonard had hoped to get Paul to accept the merely repugnant. At first the ploy failed. Paul shouted, "You're crazy." The flautist stopped again.

"Calm down. Become his writer and maybe you'll figure out how to stop him. Otherwise, there is no way. You and others will suffer."

Paul said, "I'll think about it."

"Not good enough. Listen, if you're too scared, tell him you got a friend who's twice the writer you are. Brent would dig nigger scripts—lots of sex and knife fights."

"You asshole, you win, alright, I'll play detective."

"You'll have to be like Jackie Robinson. Robinson was one tough mother, but he promised Branch Rickey not to fight if Rickey promoted him to the big leagues. The racists cursed, spat, threw fastballs at his head, but he walked away. No matter how much Brent provokes you, walk away from fights. Get him to trust you."

"Okay, and starting now, we don't know each other."

"Huh?"

"If you're right about them bugging my house, my friends are in danger. So I can't have friends. I want you healthy."

"You're going to need help."

"Yeah, but Bruce Lee is dead and Rambo's unavailable."

"Maybe you're right, but let's figure out a way to stay in touch."

"Great, we'll play spy. Tell you what, I'll put a coded want ad in the *Tribune*."

They worked out a simple code and Leonard turned to go. He took a few steps, stopped, and called back over his shoulder, "Promise me, if Brent asks you to deliver a package to me, you'll do it."

Paul stared at the receding figure, remembering how he'd introduced himself to Leonard five years earlier by asking for directions to the Berkeley library. Leonard had held up a backpack full of books. "That's just where these guys are headed. C'mon along and join us." Paul recognized a book of Barry Gifford short stories and said, "I'm a Gifford fan too." Within ten minutes they'd discovered a mutual interest in writing and made arrangements to get together for coffee. Within a month they'd become best friends. Now, standing alone on Telegraph, Paul recalled Brent's boast that he'd interfered with Paul's life weeks earlier. He'd hinted at years. And Ontological Configurations had a lifetime performance award. Paul realized that he had to reassess all his relationships, had to consider the possibility that Leonard was part of Brent's troupe. He flopped back onto the bench. *(I can't think that way. If I can't trust even Leonard, Brent's already won. I should just pack it in.)* But he had thought that way. At that moment he despised himself. He lifted himself off the bench and spat into the gutter.

Paul had no desire to rush home. Home, once a haven, a place of laughter and security, had become a site where demented people spied on him for cruel games. The flautist had an apparently inexhaustible repertoire, so he dropped a few more coins in the basket and settled in. Eventually the flow of people slowed. The flautist pocketed the money from a profitable night, put away her instrument, and offered to buy Paul a drink. He declined, then remembered that Leonard had driven. Having no car, wearing a short-sleeved shirt, he plodded home in the cold night air.

OC

On April 17, 1961, 1,400 American-trained Cuban exiles began the "Bay of Pigs" invasion of Cuba. One week earlier, President John Kennedy had said during a press conference that "...there will not be, under any conditions, an intervention in Cuba by the United States Armed Forces."

Kennedy's successor, Lyndon Johnson, campaigned actively for peace in late 1968. According to the Congressional Record, 147,786 tons of bombs were dropped over Laos during the first ten months of 1968. During the peace initiative in November and December, 91,831 tons were dropped.

Johnson's successor, Richard Nixon—enough said.

Nixon's successor, Gerald Ford, was caught in lies to the American public. As was his successor, Jimmy Carter. And his, Ronald Reagan. And his, George Bush. And Obama. And then there was Donald Trump.

Private Detection

Paul, would have preferred visiting Arlene Conant after hours but worried that a house call would put her in jeopardy. Instead, he drove to the radio station to see the large-boned, thirty-year station manager. Arlene smiled, "The prodigal son returns," and jumped up to hug him.

"Arlene, can we talk in private. I need your help."

She closed the door. "I hope you're not worrying about your future here. Terry's given some dynamite interviews as your replacement, but he's a terrible softball player."

Paul crumpled up a piece of paper and threw it at her. She squealed happily, "That's why I missed you. It's nice to be disrespected occasionally. Alright, what's your problem?"

Paul told her about Brent, Ontological Configurations, and the rest, and asked her to recommend a trustworthy police official. Arlene was well-connected. That night, one of her detective friends knocked on his door. Paul repeated the story. Detective Lenz listened sympathetically but was discouraging. "If Arlene vouches for you, that's good enough for me. I believe you. But I can't help. We have no evidence to charge him with any crime, we don't have the manpower to put him under surveillance, and I wouldn't know what to look for if we did." Paul asked for advice, and Lenz shrugged and handed him a card. "Call me if you get anything tangible."

The detective called the next day to say that he'd checked the police database. Brent had no record and was very wealthy.

Paul rented a van and parked it down the street from the house where he'd met Hal. He assumed that Brent lived there. For about thirty hours over the next five days he sat in the back in the dark, camera at the ready. Both Brent and Dominic arrived and departed several times and eleven people visited, not including a pizza delivery boy. Nobody dumped dead bodies on the front porch or brought in truckloads of arms shipments or wore signs saying "I am a Mafia don."

He called Leonard from a pay phone to ask for listings of incoming and outgoing calls from Brent's house and return addresses on all mail to there. Leonard and his network of friends came through, but Paul couldn't figure how to use the information. He called a few numbers and drove by some of the addresses but devised no strategy for documenting criminal activity. After a week he returned to work, still intent on doing something but with no plan of action.

Trajectories

Two days passed. On day three his mailbox held a clipping from the *New York Daily News*. Clayton Abrams, a twenty-year-old shipping clerk with no prior criminal or psychiatric records, was apprehended stealing kitchenware from a Salvation Army drop box. Paul assumed that Brent had sent the clipping but couldn't figure out why. The name Clayton Abrams rang no bells. Another clipping came on each of the next three days. None of the names evoked memories.

Chicago Tribune: K.D. Baines, a thirty-one-year-old attorney, had deliberately maneuvered a rented truck across two lanes of traffic on the Brooklyn Bridge during rush hour. Then he'd stopped the truck and tossed the keys into the water below. Several minor accidents and a massive traffic jam ensued.

Kansas City Star: Forty-two-year-old Colleen Boltz suffered several minor injuries including a broken wrist when she tried jumping a motorcycle over two parked cars. Boltz had never previously ridden a motorcycle. She'd bought it expressly for the attempt.

Las Vegas Review-Journal: Wealthy insurance executive Ronald Carpenter, fifty-three, became outraged upon losing twenty times in a row at a dollar slot machine. He returned to the casino the next day with a small explosive and blew up the offending machine. Two people suffered minor injuries. Carpenter was taken into police custody and had bail set at $100,000.

The fifth day's envelope contained pages 15, 40, 65, 90, and 115 from the Walnut Creek phone directory. Each page had the sixteenth name from the bottom circled: Clayton Abrams, K. Baines, Colleen Boltz, Ronald Carpenter—and Audrey Combes. The accompanying note read, "Plot the trajectories for age" (Paul's mom was sixty-four) "geographical location, and severity of consequences. Would you like to reconsider your decision about writing scripts?"

Home phone no longer trusted, Paul ran to a nearby Safeway store to check on his mother. Once she confirmed that she felt fine, he said he'd bought a plane ticket so she could visit her sister in Florida. He said he'd swung a great deal because a friend had been forced to cancel a trip. However, the ticket had to be used within the next few days. Her excitement cheered him, though he had to endure several painful questions about Marice. His mother cried when he said they'd decided not to see each other any more.

He booked a flight to Topeka. Then he called Brent and said, "I'm looking forward to start writing for you in a few days." They arranged to meet to discuss his first assignment. He said, "But I warn you, if anything happens to my mother, I'll kill you." Marice had issued a similar warning to police captain Steige concerning harm to Paul. Brent chuckled.

Paul laid a bouquet on his father's headstone, kissed it, then set down a CD player. In a conversational voice, he said, "Hi Dad, I brought your favorite. Holst's 'The Planets.' Of course, by now you'd probably be into rap." He took out a photograph in a wooden frame wrapped in a baggie and taped it onto the headstone.

"This was taken a month ago. Mom still looks great, doesn't she? Dad, my report card's not so good. I don't think you would have approved of what I'm going to do, but I can't think of anything better. I'll try to find a way out of this mess, but right now I'm stuck. I hope I never have to tell Mom. I love you."

He drove back to the airport and took the next flight to Oakland.

OC

In a 1940 book, biologist H.B. Cott drew parallels between Darwinian evolution and international arms races. Cott wrote:

> *Before asserting that the deceptive appearance of a grasshopper or butterfly is unnecessarily detailed, we must first ascertain what are the powers of perception and discrimination of the insects' natural enemies. Not to do so is like asserting that the armour of a battle cruiser is too heavy, or the range of her guns too great, without inquiring into the nature and effectiveness of the enemy's armament... Just as greater speed in the pursued has developed in relation to aggressive weapons, so the perfection of concealing devices has evolved in response to increased powers of perception.*

Some comments had been penciled in the margin of the xeroxed page.

Evoltnry arms races r costly. Biochmcl machnry used 2 locate prey or avoid predtrs is unavalbl 4 matng or resistng diseas. Somtims the cost is 2 hi.

If prey species greatly out#s preds, only small % of prey fall victm & prey nevr evolvs countrmesurs. Ex: bolas spidr dangls on strand from ovrhang and emits female moth pheromon. It swngs 2nd strand like lasso at moths flyng nerby. If spidr misses, moth typicly flies back withn range.

If pred exploits bt dosnt kill prey, prey may nevr lern.

All the OC readings had a clear theme: Deception is part of the natural order and practiced at all levels of life. Paul speculated that Brent had stumbled upon the Cott book and concluded that humans, no less than other organisms, must constantly improve their abilities at deceiving. The bolas spider example illustrated that some deceptions may never be avoided.

Don't Hit On Marice

Marice had no interest in revisiting London and rejected going anywhere that might be fun. Exile was to be endured, not enjoyed. She eventually settled on New Zealand. Once checked in at the hotel and showered, she asked for a modem hook-up:

From
"Marice Soriano" <m.soriano@hotmail.com

Date
Thursday, October 10, 2020 4:07:00 A.M.

To
"Joanna Soriano" <j.soriano@aol.com

Subject: Auckland

Hi Sweetie,
We drove through Auckland on the way to the hotel. It's gorgeous, reminds me of SF. Waitemata Harbour is more interesting than SF Bay (sacrilegious but true). My hotel (Sheraton Auckland Hotel and Towers) rates 5 stars, and they put me in the Governor Suite. Don't worry, I'm fine.

Love to everybody,
M

Brent's only restriction was that she contact no one in the U.S. other than Joanna. She put on a sweater and headed for the waterfront, where she watched tiny crabs skitter through the sand and detour around spectacularly colored, intricately coiled seashells. Their beauty almost changed her mood to nonsuicidal. Then, within a span of ten minutes, the sky changed from California blue to forbidding gray. A cold, slashing rain forced her to run the quarter-mile back to the hotel. The doorman waved her in and recommended that she go straight to the lobby to warm up with tea. She wrung out her sweater, shook her hair, and found an empty table.

"Hi, mind if I join you?"

Marice stopped sipping to look up at the speaker, a well-dressed thirtyish man with strong chin and gray sideburns.

"Thanks," she smiled, "I'd rather be alone."

Undeterred, he said "You're obviously a tourist. Kiwis know never to leave home without an umbrella during rainy season." He sat down across from her and motioned a waiter.

"Oh, and when is rainy season?"

"Roughly from September 16 to September 15 of the next year. Sometimes from April 3 to April 2 of the next year."

He laughed at his well-practiced witticism and she smiled again. Encouraged, he extended his hand. "My name is Graeme. I'm here for the travel agent's convention." They shook. "A pleasure meeting you Graeme. I've got to go now. Hubby is waiting."

Neither of them noticed the video camera with telephoto lens, a camera that also filmed Graeme later in the day struggling with two policemen as they led him away for disrupting the convention. Paul saw the video two weeks later, plus videos of other men who had approached Marice and thereby selected themselves as victims. The parts where she had declined their invitations were edited out.

Marice's stay in Auckland was cut short after only two weeks. She received a message to fly back home and report to Brent. But she had to move to the new San Francisco apartment and couldn't return yet to La Raza.

Tutorial

Paul had asked before and received an unsatisfactory answer. He tried again. "Why did two people have to die?"

"Can't let a few casualties stand in the way of creative genius."

Leonard's words about moral actions no longer seemed so repugnant. Trying to learn about Brent's methods, Paul picked up a phone directory and opened a page. "Here's a name. Elias Natowitz. Suppose your task was to get him on a plane to Rio de Janeiro. Could you do it?"

"Can a bear shit in the woods? Do you want speed or creativity?"

"Do both."

"If I had to get him to Rio before another player made him do something else, I might call and say my company was conducting a promotional campaign—he'd won an expense-free vacation, non-transferable, used immediately or void. Or I'd pose as a researcher canvassing his neighborhood for volunteers for a high-paying experiment on air travel. Or I'd show health inspector credentials and tell him that he'd been exposed to a deadly virus and needed immediate treatment—treatment available only in Rio."

"Here's an idea. You'd need even more ingenuity and creativity to persuade Irish Catholics that they don't hate Irish Protestants. Or to broker peace in the Middle East. Or to get people of different races in the U.S. to care for each other. How about setting up contests for those objectives?"

"Where's the fun? No violence, bloodshed, humiliation. To get back to Natowitz, if my goal was creativity, I'd get his vital stats: age, marital status, job, health, and so on. That would give me clues about potential rewards so I could arrange for a rich uncle he never knew to die. Or a witness who'd say she could provide evidence to save his brother from prison. Or my favorite—a gorgeous woman to come into his life." He winked. "Whatever the reward, a chain of events would end with him finding a map or photograph or newspaper column convincing him to go to Rio. If I liked Natowitz, that would be it. Otherwise, I might first get him to boo in the middle of a concert at Carnegie Hall, or paint his balls purple. Incidentally, I'm thinking of amending the rules. Wouldn't it be a kick if we told the targets ahead of time!"

OC

The following is a sample of studies conducted within the past century by reputable U.S. scientists:

A Nobel Prize winner injected live cancer cells into elderly patients without their knowledge.

To study the course of syphilis, scientists told 399 syphilitic black men that they were being given excellent medical treatment; in fact, the men were deliberately not treated. Most died prematurely, in several cases not before infecting wives and unborn babies.

A surgeon, curious about how the thymus gland affects immune response, removed the glands from eleven youngsters during heart surgery.

Male alcoholics received a drug that temporarily stops respiration. All said the experience was horrible and they thought they were dying.

Researchers injected radioactive plutonium into about 9,000 men, women, and children, including women of child-bearing age, without their knowledge. They fed dozens of retarded boys radioactive food. Human radiation tests were sponsored by the predecessors to the U.S. Energy Department, the Pentagon, and other government agencies.

In order to stsudy responses to stress, a psychologist led Army recruits to believe their plane was about to crash.

JORADIAN PAUL

BRENT HAD CALLED DANVILLE City Councilman Grady McCallum the soul mate of Callahan, Marice's London murder victim. Brent assigned the councilman to be Paul's first target. Although usually apathetic about politics and outside of McCallum's district, Paul had contributed money to his opponent's unsuccessful campaign. Having McCallum as target made the job slightly less distasteful.

Paul's assignment was to get McCallum to do a striptease with another man while a hidden camera recorded. His overriding objectives were to learn Brent's methods and capabilities and to document illegal activities. After deciding that a science fiction theme would offer the broadest possibilities, he asked if Brent's staff could doctor a newspaper or magazine that McCallum reliably read. Brent said, "Piece of cake." He assigned an operative to follow McCallum and learn his reading habits. McCallum subscribed to *The National Observer*. A special message inserted inside the next issue, skillfully placed in the middle of the lead article, read:

ATTENTION, GRADY MCCALLUM. THIS COMMUNICATION COMES FOR YOUR EYES ONLY, DIRECTLY FROM THE PLANET JORAD ON THE STAR YOU CALL ARCTURUS. OUR EXPLORERS AND SCIENTISTS HAVE SELECTED YOU TO BE OUR LIAISON WITH EARTH AND TO SHAPE OUR POLICY THERE. MEET WITH US IN ROOM 917, THE DURANT HOTEL, AT 8:00 P.M. ON

SATURDAY, SEPTEMBER 18th. YOU WILL RECEIVE A CONFIRMATORY MESSAGE AT 3:00 A.M. ON THE PRECEDING TUESDAY. NOTE WELL: NOBODY ELSE WILL RECEIVE THIS MESSAGE.

Brent said, "Writers learn best if they participate in their first script. So, I want you to direct the cast and be an actor. I won't give advice unless you ask, but talk to the technicians. They're as good as Hollywood's best and do things you wouldn't dream of—like treating the magazine with a special chemical so they can set it on fire from a distance."

Three days after finalizing the script, Brent showed Paul a videotape of McCallum buying the magazine and putting it in his attaché case; an hour later, browsing through and gasping; making an immediate phone call, then walking furiously, magazine in hand, to an office down the hall to thrust it at a fellow councilman. The friend leaned back to read and see why McCallum seemed so agitated. The magazine burst into flame, charring several documents and scarring the desk. The friend cursed while McCallum protested his innocence and said he'd pay for damages.

Brent's staff set speakers around the perimeter of McCallum's secluded estate. On Tuesday, September 14 at 3:00 A.M., they began broadcasting haunted house sounds. He hadn't been able to sleep, and he ran to the window as soon as the noises started—above, blazoned in the sky, shone his name, the name Jorad, and the words "PEACE AND FRIENDSHIP." The pilot had flown low enough to keep the skywriting out of the view of neighbors.

Room 917 of the Durant has a skylight. The staff had calculated carefully, arranging for the meeting on a date when the moon would be waning. They could position a video camera above the skylight that could scan the entire room and be almost impossible to detect. They set a second camera behind a spy hole in an adjacent room. Paul planned to insist that McCallum strip to prove to the "Joradian" (Paul) that he had come unarmed. Paul would also strip, each taking off one item in turn until both were naked. (Brent had acceded to Paul's demand that his face remain disguised.) Brent's men would burst in pretending to be hotel detectives. McCallum would probably try to pull rank and demand that they question Paul, but he'd be escorted outside, forcibly if necessary. He'd be completely baffled about what had happened—until the video appeared on local television stations.

The crew arrived several hours early to costume Paul in the hotel room rather than having to sneak him upstairs in full regalia. Brent's make-up artists made him look distinctly otherworldly. His skin had a purplish tint, and a rubber appendage attached to his navel could be wriggled in interesting ways.

Camera noises were masked by Sitar music piped through a hidden speaker. Brent's set designers strung up psychedelic lights, apparently under the directive that the planet Jorad resembled Berkeley of the 1960s. As an added touch, they smeared essence of durian over Paul's body. The essence, sold in Oakland's Chinatown, comes from a large fruit loved by Indonesians but so notoriously foul-smelling that it's banned on Indonesian buses. The make-up artists ignored Paul's protest, insisting that the smell would convince McCallum of Paul's extraterrestrial origin.

So he waited—hungry, sweat pooling inside the heavy costume, nausea growing with each respiration. Still, though he disliked playing the kind of role usually reserved for prostitutes and cheap private investigators, he wanted the plan to work. He'd brought along a deck of cards and dealt out a game of solitaire.

Many games later, at 8:15, the door thumped. Paul waddled over to slide open the bolt and croaked "Please come in" in what he hoped was a sufficiently unique accent. A gargantuan head poked inside. Seeing only one weirdly costumed individual, he shoved the door inward with hurricane force, propelling Paul backwards onto the bed. The six feet, seven inches, 350-pound hurricane stormed in, waving a superfluous gun. He commanded Paul not to move. "Looks like he's alone, boss," he shouted down the hallway. An answering voice said, "Okay boys, find out what the hell is going on."

Three more large armed men rushed inside, McCallum trailing. Paul had the frightening realization that the film crew was powerless to intervene. McCallum snarled "Who's paying you?" while one of the men pointed a gun and the others ransacked the room.

Paul just grunted. McCallum ordered the men to strip him. "Get that shit off. Let's see who's under there." They pulled buttons and zippers, then one man ripped into the costume with a knife. Another stood on a chair and reported that nobody was on the other side of the skylight. Relieved that the crew had escaped, Paul lay naked, trapped with five armed, angry, and almost certainly dangerous people. His best hope was to stall until a crew member summoned help.

"He's not wired and doesn't have a gun, Mr. McCallum."

While his men restrained Paul's arms and legs, McCallum prodded his face. He stretched an ear, spit into it, said, "You're on the clock. Two minutes. Talk or you're going to be severely damaged."

"By the laws of the Third Intergalactic Federation, you are required to treat me humanely. I don't have to tell you anything except my name, genus, and planetary cluster."

Wisecracking was the wrong response. One man cuffed his head and another volunteered, "Mr. McCallum, why don't the rest of you leave and let me waste this doofus."

McCallum paused to consider, then stiffened as he heard distant police sirens. They might have been heading for the hotel. "Naw, I'm in politics to help people, not hurt them."

To Paul, "Listen creep, I don't know what your game is. I'm not going to do anything this time, but pull another prank like this and you're dead. Let's go boys."

They started to leave, taking his costume with them. Then, almost as an afterthought, McCallum said, "Marlin, looks like the creep's got a damaged finger. Why don't you let him have a matching pair."

Brent arrived about ten minutes later carrying a pair of bright red Bermuda shorts several sizes too large for Paul and a garish Hawaiian shirt. Faced with the alternative of walking naked through the lobby, Paul draped them on. In the street, Joradian facial make-up still partially in place, right index finger in a splint and left one cocked at a strange angle, he attracted the stares of even the most jaded Berkeley pedestrians. Brent opened the limo door and said he regretted how the night had turned out. His eyes twinkled.

"Then why did you let me go through with it?"

"Baptism by fire. I wanted you to learn that mistakes can be costly, even fatal. You're not dealing with fraternity boys."

"What went wrong?"

Brent sighed, exasperated teacher to considerably less than sterling new pupil: "One, Grady McCallum is a hard-nosed practical politician. Two, he's made a career of hating non-Aryans. I doubt that he has any blond, *green-eyed* people on his staff. Now what in hell's name made you think he would go up to some strange hotel room to conduct a civilized meeting with creatures from another solar system?"

"I guess that was too much to ask for."

"Too much to ask for!" Brent accompanied his echo with rolling eyes. "McCallum's a consistent winner in a cut-throat profession. He's been in office for seven years and got sixty-two percent of the votes last time. The man is not stupid. He'd be a great scriptwriter."

"Then make him an offer," Paul screamed in a voice that came out much higher pitched than intended. He banged on the window. "Stop the car! Let me out!" He'd had enough. Anyone who spoke disrespectfully again or put a hand on him in other than the friendliest of contexts would have hell to pay. He intended to restore his dignity.

They discharged him in downtown Oakland, where dignity-restoration proved problematic. With two damaged hands dangling, he had a difficult time even holding up the monstrous shorts. Midnight is a dangerous time to be walking unarmed in the squalid MacArthur Boulevard area, but people gave him a wide berth except for three teenage boys. They asked if he was an actor and looked around for cameras and crew. One took off his headphones and said, "Creature-man be goin' to meet Calvin's momma." The shortest of the three, obviously Calvin, retorted, "Creature-man pimpin' for Melvin's momma." The third reached into his jacket and pulled out a flask containing some alcoholic beverage. He gingerly offered it to Paul, seeking to establish rapport with the strange beast. Paul accepted the flask and took a swig. They laughed, and he gave a Joradian bellow. They weren't fooled any more than McCallum had been, but the masquerade livened up what had until then been a boring night. One of them eventually convinced the others that Paul was on a special vice squad detail. Each slapped his hand in comradely fashion. They left wondering aloud about the nature of the pervert who would accept him as bait.

Kaiser is big and impersonal, but Paul had become a familiar presence. The intake clerk called for his chart and said with a barely muffled laugh, "Basketball is sure tough on the old bod."

Paralegal

Paul eased himself into bed trying not to put pressure on any of his sore spots, and Colombo jumped on the covers to curl up against him. Paul stroked the cat's soft fur, glad for the companionship—the only companion who was safe around him. Two thoughts dominated his thinking: Marice had left forever, and Brent hadn't. Colombo extended his neck and purred when Paul dutifully scratched. The purrs changed to rhythmic breathing. Paul envied the cat's ability to sleep. Hours later sleep overcame him as well, and he made love with Marice. But just before climax he heard a bell and looked up. Brent, Venn, Hal, and a squirrel, like judges at an Olympic gymnastics event, each held a card with a number rating his lovemaking. His scores were low.

Though certain that Brent would eventually reestablish contact and inflict further misery, Paul could think of nothing short of murder to forestall him. He worried that petting Colombo, brushing his teeth, making coffee—every move he made—earned points for Brent. He opened his laptop but the writing tap was dry, so he switched from word processing to backgammon. He beat the computer, played again and lost, played again, played again. He emptied the week-old sugar water from the hummingbird feeder and poured in a new supply, switched back to word processing, still couldn't write. In the middle of his fifteenth backgammon game, as he considered whether to accept a double, the phone rang.

"Hello."

"Hi Paulie, it's your mom." Her tone signaled exciting news. "I just met a friend of yours."

His adrenals started their now daily surge. "Aunt Ida and I were strolling along the beach, and a man asked for directions. Before Ida answered, he asked if I used to live in Kansas. Then he asked, 'Do you have a son named Paul?' He's a lot older than you but says he knows you well and even called himself your mentor. His name is Brent Willerman. I was embarrassed at not remembering. He left his phone number and asked me to have you call him. He said the two of you had a secret slogan, 'Remember the trajectories,' whatever that means."

Like a master fisherman, Brent had allowed Paul to briefly pull away and then drawn the line taut. Paul urged his mother to extend her visit. "Stay awhile, you see Aunt Ida so rarely." Distance obviously did not present a serious barrier to Brent, but Paul hoped he'd want his workforce back in Oakland. He called the fisherman.

"Brent, if anything happens to my mother I'll kill you."

"You've told me. I've slept with one eye open ever since."

"I mean it."

"Listen old buddy, what happened with McCallum was my fault. I threw you in over your head. Why don't you try again at a noncompetitive event."

"I'm listening."

"A guy I know is a defense lawyer. He's lazy and no great intellect, but he wins more than he loses. He makes up good stories about what his client was doing on the night of the crime and can usually convince at least one juror that his guy couldn't have done it."

"How do I fit in?"

"His job is like a script writer's, only with smaller stakes—a paycheck and the freedom of some scumball. Work with him on his next case. He helps train my people, and in exchange they do free legwork for him. Figure out why he does so well."

"How can you call a trial noncompetitive?"

"I meant, the outcome makes no difference."

The defendant was a young Vietnamese man accused of shooting and killing a jewelry store owner during a robbery. That's a capital offense in California. The jeweler's assistant and a customer picked Victor Hoang out of a line-up after his capture three hours later. Hoang belonged to a gang and had a criminal record. His left arm sported a tattoo of a bloody dagger. The attorney encouraged Paul to use his creative skills to concoct a plausible alibi. "It'll be a good learning experience. Don't worry if you fuck up. I get paid by the hour and the guilty son-of-a-bitch deserves to die."

Paul read over the statements of police and witnesses, visited the store, and interviewed Hoang and friends. The cumulative information convinced him, to his considerable surprise, that Hoang was innocent. Four compelling pieces of evidence stood out.

1. Neither of the two Caucasian witnesses had had a good look at the murderer. They made contradictory initial statements and admitted talking with one of Hoang's policeman captors just prior to viewing the line-up.

2. The crime had been committed on a rainy day. Muddy footprints in the store were two sizes larger than Hoang's shoe size.

3. One of Hoang's friends swore they had burglarized a house together at the time of the murder. Police records confirmed that the house, thirty miles away from the jewelry store, had been burglarized on that date. Hoang's friend showed Paul the loot. Though he faced a prison sentence if charged and convicted, he signed a confession to the burglary.

4. In a separate incident, the police raided a pawn shop and confiscated the inventory. It included the stolen jewelry. The pawn shop owner confessed to buying it from a Vietnamese man three days after Hoang's capture. The fence, according to the owner's description, was of about the same height and build as Hoang.

Paul sat in a front-row seat in the courtroom and listened in frustration as the bored attorney presented an uninspiring defense. Still, the compelling exculpatory evidence made the prosecution's closing remarks seem like desperate grasps at straws. The prosecutor suggested that Hoang might have given the jewelry to somebody before he was caught, deliberately worn oversize shoes to confuse police, and paid the friend to testify. The friend was called a habitual criminal and non-credible witness; and the grieving widow and her two young children sat facing the jury each day. After two hours of deliberation, the jury returned a verdict of guilty.

Brent hailed Paul as he left the courthouse trailing Hoang's stunned and dejected relatives and friends. "Hey dickhead, oh for two. That chink's gonna fry." He laughed and stuck out his tongue toward a slightly built Vietnamese man. The man shouted something in Vietnamese. Brent yelled, "Hey chink, who you looking at?" The entire group surged forward. Dominic shoved away the closest man, and two policemen on their way to court rushed over to break up the incipient fight. A thrown stick fell harmlessly several feet from Brent. He laughed until tears streamed from his eyes and he began coughing. Recovering, he turned to Paul and asked, "Do you want to try again?"

"I have no choice. But do me a favor. Hoang is innocent. Get him a real lawyer and file an appeal."

"Yeah, okay. Society needs more like him on the streets. I'll see that he gets off to fulfill his destiny. C'mon over to poolside at the Claremont Hotel tomorrow and let's talk."

MEETING THE SERVANT GIRL

THE STATELY CLAREMONT HAD survived Oakland's big fire only because of a fortuitous last minute change in the wind. Paul weaved his way through the opulent foyer to the huge pool in back. Brent looked up from a large recliner and waved him over. "Isn't life great," he said, hoisting a pitcher. "I see that the splints are off your hands. That's wonderful." He filled two glasses. "Bourbon over ice. Just the thing for a hot day." He pushed a glass toward Paul. "Tell me, what did you learn from the trial?"

"Not much. Justice isn't colorblind. But I already knew that."

"Now listen up while I dispense wisdom. What you should have learned is that juries aren't swayed by logic."

"Next time I'll bring Tarot cards."

"Stop being such a sarcastic prick. If arguments were decided logically, philosophers would be useful. But abstractions don't win, emotion does. Juries fall asleep during fingerprint and DNA testimony. They wake up to see the widow and her little girls and vote guilty. Want a great example of the irrelevance of logic? A supreme example? Watch our Supreme Court in action. The justices know before they ever hear an argument how they're going to vote. At the end of the day, no matter what they had heard, brilliant Thurgood Marshall voted for civil rights and brilliant Antonin Scalia said 'Fry the sonofabitch.'"

Paul frowned. He'd once made a similar point on the show and hated being in agreement with Brent about anything. Also, although his current role was thoroughly distasteful, he hated that Brent's competence so exceeded his own. Brent continued,

"Look, suppose you prove that if I accept A and B, C follows automatically. Nice, neat, QED. But suppose I don't accept A or B. McCallum didn't accept your bullshit story and the jury disbelieved your evidence. That, my man, is how the world works."

"So, the trick is to find the right starting points."

"Bingo. But what's obvious to you might seem stupid to a woman or Mexican or old person. You believe in God. Millions of people don't. Bertrand Russell and Einstein didn't. Were they dumber than you? You think democracy is great. Plato would have called you an asshole. You think the sun will rise tomorrow. Some physicist or Army general may know better."

Brent emptied the pitcher and picked up a walkie-talkie to order more bourbon and ice. Paul covered the mouthpiece with his hand. "I know you have people who live just so they can serve you, but I'm capable of walking fifty feet to the bar."

"Sit down, we've got a new target to discuss. Besides, my personal staff really do love waiting on me. They'd be offended if I let you go."

"A little exercise would do you good." Paul stayed in his chair but draped a towel over his head so he didn't have to watch the groveling deliverer of drinks. "Sun's in my eyes," he said.

"Does the name Corby Quinn mean anything to you?"

It did. Quinn had been charged two years earlier with the rape and murder of a young woman. His trial kept news of global warming, acid rain, political corruption, various wars, civil disturbances, and an earthquake off the front pages of local papers for about a month. Soon after his acquittal a reporter uncovered incontrovertible evidence that key witnesses had perjured themselves. But nothing could be traced directly to Quinn, and the D.A. concluded that a retrial would be pointless. The Quinn case made an interesting counterpoint to Hoang's. Quinn made money off a ghostwritten biography, and a coast guard crew discovered the reporter floating face down in the bay.

"Are you asking me to get Quinn?"

"My task is to send him on a long and fruitless journey."

"He's in big trouble." Paul emphasized the word 'big.' His rage needed an outlet, and for the time being Brent was invulnerable. Quinn would be a welcome surrogate. He leaned back in the lounge chair, towel over his head, while children squealed and splashed nearby. Someone approached clinking ice cubes. Brent tapped his shoulder and said, "The bourbon's here."

"I don't want any."

Brent tapped again. "You'll have plenty of time for Quinn. Take off the towel."

Paul reluctantly sat up and opened his eyes. Directly in front of him, dazzlingly beautiful in a French maid's outfit, stood Marice. She smiled politely, as though he were a former high school teacher dimly remembered as kindly but dull. Brent snapped her bra string. "I forgot, you two know each other." She patted Brent's belly, and a taste of vomit welled up in Paul's throat.

"You'll probably want to discuss old times. But give me a little longer. Paul needs some guidance." He spun her around and dismissively patted her bottom.

(*Remember Jackie Robinson.*) Paul muttered, "You bastard," innocuous enough under the circumstances.

"I am, I love it. Isn't life great." Brent's round face bobbed gleefully. "Now listen up while I give you some tips."

Marice went to the room number stamped on Brent's key. The closet held three blouses, a skirt, pants, shoes, and underwear, all new, all the right sizes. She changed and scribbled the note according to instructions.

B. Have to pick some things up for tonite. Ironed your blue shirt & hung it in closet. Tell Paul I'm sorry we didn't get a chance to chat. M

She placed the note on the bed and called for a cab. Then she called Joanna and asked if they could meet at Macy's. When she and her sister were alone, she said, "Here's what I need you to do."

Paul forced himself to look attentive while Brent dispensed advice on scriptwriting. Brent told him to read psychiatry texts to learn about the belief systems of paranoid psychotics. Paranoids, he said, are notoriously hard to treat because they typically have highly coherent belief systems. The paranoid starts with some bizarre premise such as that little green men are out to get him, then interprets everything that happens to preserve the "truth" of that premise. Once it's accepted, all else follows logically. If Ann believes that Bob hates her and Bob invites her to dinner, she may conclude that he intends to rape or poison her.

Brent told Paul about an incident in New York about twenty years earlier. A young man boarded a crowded subway train, screamed "Death to all bugs!" and sprayed insecticide throughout the car. The passengers panicked, thinking it was poison gas. Transit police subdued the man and took him to a psychiatric ward, where he was assigned to a psychiatrist named Klemmer. During the intake interview, he repeatedly asserted that all insects were directed by a single powerful insect mind that would eventually annihilate the human species.

The patient scored at the genius level on an IQ test and awed Klemmer with his knowledge of and passion for insects. Klemmer began extending their fifty-minute sessions into entire mornings. At lunchtimes, Klemmer ate alone while poring over entomology texts. He neglected other patients. Four months later, he burst into the hospital cafeteria, shouted "Death to all bugs!" and sprayed insecticide at his startled colleagues. Brent said that dozens of psychiatrists had been similarly sucked into their patients' delusional systems.

Brent said, "Remember I told you that psychiatric residents at Langley Porter used to take LSD as part of their training. Acid creates new realities. Supposedly normal people start thinking they can fly or talk to God or see molecules whizzing around inside a leaf. You and me together, we'll be stronger than acid."

Then he said words that Paul yearned to hear—and dreaded. "You're probably tired of all this heavy stuff. I'll call the servant girl so you two can reminisce. Order anything you want. Put it on my tab."

The 'servant girl' didn't answer the walkie-talkie. Brent said, "Here's the key to our room ('our room'—the words elicited a fresh taste of vomitus). She's a heavy sleeper. If she doesn't answer the bell, let yourself in."

Paul turned the key. Nobody was there—just an open closet of women's clothing and the note.

First Successful Script

Paul consoled himself with the thought that Corby Quinn, probably even more than McCallum, deserved victimhood. Quinn lived alone in a large ranch style home in the Oakland Hills with a spectacular panoramic view of the bay. Partly because of the publicity generated by his trial, partly because of his general lifestyle, he'd installed a sophisticated security system. A ten-feet gate surrounded the house, and security cameras covered the entire grounds. Two pit bulls roamed free. Undeterred, Paul worked out a plan that Brent praised, calling it a big improvement over the previous one. Despite himself, Paul was pleased.

Brent's network of low-level criminals put word out on the street that the perpetrators of a multimillion-dollar diamond robbery in South Africa had escaped to the tiny African republic of Burundi. Although the robbery had gone smoothly, their fence had been arrested in an unrelated incident. Desperate to sell their haul, the perpetrators would accept five cents on the dollar plus help in relocating to England or the U.S. Quinn received assurances that he could get the diamonds through customs. Just a quick in/out, no risk, and a profit of millions.

As anticipated, Quinn didn't trust anybody else to carry the cash or retrieve the diamonds. He flew to Bujumbura International Airport and checked the money-filled suitcase into a secure safe in Bujumbura's best hotel. Then he showed the desk clerk a map indicating his destination. The clerk tried to dissuade him, but he'd already flown 10,000 miles and would not turn back empty-handed. The clerk explained that Burundi's Tutsi and

Hutu tribes were in the midst of a deadly civil war. Nobody was safe, and even Bujumbura might be evacuated. Quinn insisted until the clerk dispatched an underling to locate a guide.

The two men trudged five miles across difficult terrain, barely speaking, until they reached a small hill marked by a row of recently-turned mounds of soil. The guide said, "Much fighting here. I go no more." He pointed to the southwest and said, "Four more kilometers." Quinn pleaded for the guide to continue, but he turned toward home. Quinn wavered, started going on alone, then heard a burst of gunfire followed by several blood-curdling screams. He caught up with the guide and returned to the U.S. with no diamonds and a severe case of malaria.

Brazilian Update

Brent congratulated Paul on the Quinn success. He added, "Remember the man whose name you picked out of the phonebook? I followed up. Two months ago he was managing a successful real estate agency in Oakland. I'm sending an update."

The next day's mail included a picture of a smiling bespectacled man in a park, surrounded by laughing children. A note was attached:

> *Dear Monsignor Willerman,*
>
> *Although we've never met, I owe you a great deal. Your overwhelming generosity has enriched my life. These kids are so needy, so loving. I will do my best to be your worthy successor. From all of us, God bless you.*
>
> *Yours, with highest esteem,*
>
> *Elias Natowitz*

Paul took a closer look at the envelope. The unusual stamp was Brazilian, the postmark from Rio. He bit his tongue but couldn't keep from laughing.

Prolific Scriptwriter

Brent said that the Quinn script had established Paul as a big leaguer, and Paul responded that big leaguers should have privileges. He requested a voice in picking future targets. Brent surprisingly assented, so Paul began a daily ritual of scouring newspapers to identify other McCallums and Quinns. He asked Arlene's contacts in the D.A.'s office if they knew any violent criminals who had been saved from prison either by judicial error or incompetent prosecutors, and who would probably commit more such crimes in the future. All responded with incredulity that anyone could be naive enough to ask. They knew dozens. Two assistant D.A.s let him see confidential case material. After one short reading session, he almost forgave himself for his new job. He disapproved of vigilante justice, but only because vigilantes rarely enact safeguards to protect the innocent; a conscientious vigilante such as himself could mete out warranted punishment indefinitely.

Paul received a new case about every three weeks and became adept at developing workable, creative scripts. Brent sent him regular checks plus videotapes of each climactic scene. He never watched them. The money, including occasional bonuses, comforted him, suggesting that Brent wasn't planning immediate violence against him or his mother. He donated the checks to Glide Memorial Church.

Brent refused to divulge the names of other players, though he enjoyed discussing other aspects of the game. He made his *Soldier of Fortune* magazine collection available. Each issue contained ads for deactivating alarm systems, opening houses and safes, secretly recording telephone and other conversations, obtaining official documents, forging documents, and filming behaviors from a distance. Paul ordered a miniature camera and tape recorder.

He asked how Brent recruited staff.

"It just takes the right bait." Brent withdrew a photograph from a nearby drawer and thrust it into Paul's face: Hal, reclining on a sofa in red bikini panties.

"I tap phones, have people followed, pay off co-workers. I've put *Soldier of Fortune* gadgets in confession boxes, judges' chambers, psychotherapists' offices, executive washrooms, and under beds in fancy hotels. Confidential secretaries and high-class hookers report to me. I run a detective agency. People actually pay me to hear their shit."

"So you see people's dirty linen. Big deal."

"Man, didn't college teach you didley-squat? They'd do anything to keep it hidden. What if he's cheated on his wife or income taxes or exams. Lied on a resume. Used illegal drugs. Been caught shoplifting. Taken a bribe. Bought stolen goods. Had a face lift, wears a toupee. Maybe he's done time in a mental hospital or prison. Has a foot fetish. I'll bet even you—saintly Paul—have done things that would stop you from casting the first stone."

More than one incident flashed through Paul's mind. "You blackmail them."

"Sure. Stamp collectors get nothing but stamps. Collectors of secrets get live people. I've got enough to invade a small country."

Paul's preferred source for prospective targets was the steady stream from the prosecutors' lists, but he also used local media. A *Tribune* reporter wrote about a hospital administrator who refused admittance to a man grievously wounded with a gunshot, because the man had no money or health insurance. Another column cited unnamed but reliable sources claiming that a superior court judge had taken a bribe to give only one year's probation to a convicted producer of child porn films.

Blackmail and intimidation were the foundation of Brent's methods for recruiting staff, but the actual games required more complex stratagems. Brent gave Paul videos of failing and barely passable efforts but refused to let him see the exceptional ones. He worried that they'd stifle Paul's creativity.

- An elderly woman fell in front of a target and strewed the contents of her shopping bag on the ground. He helped her pick up the items, each chosen to show fingerprints, each transported shortly afterwards to a crime scene. He was convicted.
- A handsome, articulate, elegantly dressed, and apparently wealthy young man contrived to encounter a middle-aged, happily married woman with two children. He claimed a powerful attraction and pursued relentlessly. He eventually charmed her into an affair and then proposed marriage. Once she'd told her bewildered husband that she wanted a trial separation, the young man disappeared never to be seen by her again.
- Firemen rushed to the porn judge's house to extinguish a fire of suspicious origin. They discovered 100 grams of cocaine in a bedroom. The judge swore he'd never seen any of it before, but the jury didn't believe him. (The porn producer didn't fare well either.)
- Brent's computer whiz altered the hospital administrator's army and college records, giving him a dishonorable discharge and taking away a degree. Paul had met the whiz, Lucien Sartie, at Hal's. (The story about the wounded person was buried in the back of the *Trib* but the scandal made its front page.)

Brent said, "*Soldier of Fortune* advertisers sell to anyone. I want cutting edge and exclusive. One of my boys keeps me updated on the latest scientific advances, like miniature implants for monitoring heart rate, blood pressure, brain activity, whatever, in animals." He winked. "Or people. Some devices won't be available to *Soldier of Fortune* readers for another decade, some you can't even imagine. Maybe that coffee you're drinking or this morning's newspaper put a chemical into your bloodstream that lights up your brain for a game player 1,000 miles away."

Paul added the *National Enquirer* and similar tabloids to his reading list. From his new perspective, he speculated about the real stories behind headlines such as "LIZARD CREATURES IN FLYING SAUCER HOLD MAN CAPTIVE FOR THREE WEEKS" and "GOD TELLS PREACHER TO RAISE 10 MILLION DOLLARS" and "SPIRIT OF DEAD UNCLE COMMANDED HER TO..."

Paul's spy gear enabled him to secretly take pictures and record conversations, but Brent didn't do anything self-incriminating in his presence. Paul requested another chance at McCallum, and the much stronger second script worked to perfection. McCallum no longer corrupts the people of Danville.

Physical expressions affect mood: Research volunteers who followed instructions to smile rated themselves as happier than previously, whereas voluntary frowners reported increased sadness. Maybe constantly walking with head turned down to shield one's face from rain promotes depression. California's 2020 winter set records for wetness, and the incessantly gray skies cast an appropriate backdrop for Paul's increasingly darkening mood. Whatever the reason, Paul's mood grew dark. Hearing nonstop Christmas music and seeing festive decorations in stores and homes didn't help. Brent's willingness to let him choose targets made the script-writing job bearable, and at times he even thought of himself as a force for good. But his criterion for success had become the effectiveness with which he inflicted pain and suffering. Although some people deserve to die and many decent citizens support capital punishment, he couldn't bring himself to believe that a decent person would apply for a job as executioner. His life was a shambles. He missed Leonard and other friends but scrupulously avoided them. He thought constantly of Marice and didn't date. He lost his light touch with radio guests, and his writing turned somber. Dostoevsky became his bedtime reading companion.

They met at the Claremont's Sunday brunch buffet to discuss the next script. Brent waved Paul over from his seat and pointed to the tables bulging with assortments of salads, eggs, sausages, breads, and desserts. "See, like I told you, best Sunday brunch in the Bay area. Grab a plate."

While Brent eradicated his mountain of food, Paul poked holes in the sunnyside-up eggs and watched the yolks yellow his plate.

"C'mon, eat. Buffets are for stuffing yourself. I'll have to double my Tums ration tonight, but it's worth it."

Brent's presence destroyed his appetite. "Tell me about the next assignment."

"Sure. By the way, have you seen Marice lately?"

"No."

"I thought she would have called you by now. I'll remind her. Unfortunately, she's forbidden me to give her number. Men pester her so much."

He bit his tongue. (*Jackie R., Jackie R.*) Brent said, "The next script is a free-form. Everybody gets a different task for Jackson Pettis, the Walnut Creek city councilman. Our job is to get him to jump on the field during a Raiders game and bark like a dog."

"I thought I could pick targets. Pettis is a decent man."

"We haven't picked any high-profile, interesting targets lately. Besides, Pettis is scum."

"He's mediocre, no worse than most politicians. I won't help destroy his career."

Brent dropped his voice, "The most severe punishments should be dealt to the mediocre. Dullness is a worse crime than murder." Chortling, "Gawd, I'm deep. Tell you what, take a holiday. I'll do Pettis myself."

Two days later, Paul found a note under his door: Call Orinda Hospital and ask for room 409.

Many Walnut Creek emergency cases are taken to nearby Orinda Hospital. Silently praying "Don't let it be Mom," he punched in the numbers.

"Orinda Hospital, information desk."

"Please tell me the name of the patient in room 409."

"Just a moment, I'll check." A few seconds later, prayer unanswered, "Audrey Combes."

"I'm her son. What's wrong?"

The receptionist connected him with a floor nurse. "She was mugged and suffered a minor concussion. She's not in any danger. She's sleeping comfortably—the doctor gave her something to help. But she'll probably have a headache tomorrow."

Paul drove to Orinda and sneaked up to her room. She was breathing regularly, head swaddled in bandages. He scribbled on a scrap of paper, "Mom, I love you, see you in the morning," and put it on her nightstand.

Muggings in the Bay Area are as common as sunsets, but the motive behind hers was unique. Paul blamed himself for not writing a script for Pettis. The next morning, he drove back to the hospital and was relieved to see his mother sitting up eating breakfast.

He squeezed her hand. "Mom, how do you feel?"

Feebly, "Hello, Paulie. That was so sweet of you to come last night. The flowers are gorgeous. I'm fine, just a bit dizzy. The doctor says I can leave today."

He rubbed his hand across her cheek. "Oh, Mom, that's a nasty bruise."

"I was walking back from the library when a nicely dressed man asked for the time. Then he said, 'Is your name Audrey?' I asked how he knew. He said, 'I have a present for you.' Then he punched me in the face. He picked me off the ground, smiled calm as day, and said, 'Bye, Audrey, send Paul my best wishes.' Then he strolled away."

He rubbed her cold hands between his own. "Mom, a very bad person is angry with me. He hurt you to get at me. I'll be able to work things out, but as soon as you're released I want you to take another trip. I'll write and explain everything."

He enlisted Arlene's help. They drove to the hospital separately and met in room 409. They exited together, Arlene walking unsteadily with head swaddled in bandages, Paul holding her hand. She checked out as Audrey Combes and drove home with him. The real Audrey, holding a plane ticket to Oahu and a suitcase full of clothing, took a taxi to the airport fifteen minutes later.

Honorable Brent

Paul asked to meet the next night, said he'd changed his mind and would do the Pettis script.

"Sure, come on over. You know my address, it's where you trysted with Hal."

"Trysted with Hal!" Even in light conversation, Brent's actions made Leonard's murder suggestion more palatable.

Dominic ushered him to a living room much less cluttered than on Paul's previous visit. Two large landscapes struck him as tasteful rather than gaudy, and a plush white carpet covered the floor. Brent said, "Dominic, take our guest's food and drink order. And put on some music. Make sure it's not Johnny Mathis."

When they were comfortably seated, Brent said, "I'm glad you're going to take on Pettis. He's too soft on crime. An elderly woman got mugged in his district in broad daylight yesterday. She survived, fortunately, but it coulda been a lot worse."

(*Robinson, Robinson, Robinson.*) Paul whispered, "There's no excuse for what you did."

"You're right, I apologize. I'm having a wide screen TV delivered to her apartment tomorrow."

"Stay away from my mother and friends."

"It's a deal."

"I'm warning you, no repeats. No more innocent victims."

"You referring to Marvin and Donna? Grow up, move on."

"Why did you kill them?"

Brent shrugged, "Stop making such a big deal of it. You think life is sacred, but people are shit and the world's overpopulated."

"Would they still be alive if I'd delivered the packages?"

"Of course. I'm an honorable man. But someone you know would have gone down eventually. Had to show you I meant business. Now, sit down, take off your jacket, and have a drink."

"I can't stay. The paper said that Marvin left a wife and two kids. Indulge me and send them enough money to live on?"

"Done. Okay, enough reminiscing. We've already lost a day on Pettis. Let's catch up."

Marice Takes a Gamble

Marice decided to defy Brent's warning. Defiance entailed risk, slight to her and substantial to Paul, but passivity hadn't improved matters. She enlisted Arturo's help once again.

Confession

Paul ran into the house and tossed his jacket onto the floor and shirt on top. Colombo appeared, yawning. Paul ignored the cat, who meowed plaintively at the appalling treatment. In one swift movement Paul ripped the thick band of tape from his waist and extracted the tiny recorder. He pressed 'Rewind,' then 'Play,' and heard his voice, "Why did you kill them?" He bellowed over the playback, "Got you, you bastard" and scratched Colombo's neck while grasping the phone with the other hand.

"Hello, Detective Lenz, this is Arlene Conant's friend Paul. You said I should call if I got any evidence. I have a confession."

Lenz's house, about a half mile below the top of the Berkeley hills, was situated along the same route that Paul and Marice had driven on the way to the behavior station. Paul noted the Maybeck and the Julia Morgan.

Lenz's wife, a pretty woman with short-cropped blonde hair, answered the door in a terrycloth bathrobe. "Excuse my outfit," she giggled. "We were cleaning downstairs." She led Paul onto the living room deck to marvel at the view. As she stirred sugar into a pitcher of iced tea, Lenz, in matching bathrobe, raced up the steps. Mr. weighed about twice as much as Mrs. "Hi Paul, excuse the bathrobe, I was exercising." He stuck out his hand. "So you got a confession. I hope you used a cattle prod."

Paul grinned proudly. "Just a little subterfuge. Maybe I'll donate a cattle prod to his future cell mates." He put the recorder on the table and pressed 'Play.' Lenz immediately shook his head from side to side, and Paul realized that optimism had been premature. Lenz said, "You were shrewd to record him saying those things, and if I'd had any doubts before, I'm 100% convinced now. But the tape wouldn't cause his lawyers to lose sleep, and no prosecutor would even indict. In fact, the one prosecutable offense is what you did. You recorded the conversation without his knowledge, and that's a felony."

Love Letter in a Gun Store

As soon as can opener touched can, Colombo sprang from his vantage point on the bedroom windowsill and rushed to the cat dish. He waited while Paul spooned out a turkey and giblets feast and poured fresh water into a bowl. With head deep in the dish, he barely heard Paul say, "Hey fat boy, don't worry about me, I'll be careful. We know you're too spoiled to survive on your own."

Colombo didn't offend easily. He cleaned his plate, stretched, rolled over, and arched his neck so Paul could scratch. Paul poured a cup of coffee and sat down to read the *Tribune*, and Colombo jumped up for his daily lap time. Leonard had steadfastly refused to address Colombo by proper name, calling him 'tumor' because of his seemingly permanent attachment to Paul's lap. Paul noticed a small cut on Colombo's nose, so he dampened a washcloth and wiped it. "Hope you got the other guy."

Flea comb in one hand, *Trib* in the other, he turned the pages aimlessly, unable to immerse himself in worldwide troubles with his own life in such turmoil. Then he noticed an advertisement for a gun store on East 14th Street. He'd never handled a gun but was sure he could learn enough to do what was necessary. He put Colombo down and drove to East 14th, oblivious to the black Honda Accord that had been parked two houses down and started up at the same time as the Prius.

Its enormity surprised him. Rows of stacked rifles, glistening pistols, gold-handled antiques locked up in display cabinets, separate areas for Uzis and clones, German guns, Russian guns, designer guns, stun guns, a bargain table, and cartons of bullets—an eclectic house of destruction with a small section in the back for bows and arrows, swords, scimitars, and daggers. He counted four clerks and two security guards. There were too many customers to count.

He found a gun on the bargain table small enough to be hidden in a pants pocket. A salesman handed him a form for a background check and said there would be a seven-day waiting period. Worried about losing nerve unless he acted immediately, Paul apologized for wasting the salesman's time and walked toward the exit. A thin Latino man tapped his shoulder. "Excuse me sir, I think you lost this." He held out a folded sheet of paper. Paul said he didn't think so, but the man insisted. Paul shrugged and unfolded the paper on his way to the car. The other man walked to his Accord.

Dear Paul,

Do NOT try to find me, but trust me, I love you and hated what happened the last time we saw each other. If I hadn't done what Brent said, he would have killed you. It probably wasn't necessary to have my friend get you this note in such a sneaky way, but he might be having both of us followed. I'm totally paranoid. If he asks you to take a lie detector test, you must find an excuse to get out of it. DO NOT UNDER ANY CIRCUMSTANCES TAKE THE TEST.

We've got to find a way to defeat him.

I miss you terribly and can't wait for the day when we can go alien hunting again.

Love,
Marice

Sweeter words he'd never read.

Rehab Center

Paul devised a new plan for getting a gun, although he hadn't figured out the step afterwards. The *Yellow Pages* listed several "Drug abuse and addiction treatment centers." He drove to the closest one, on Foothill and 35th Street. A radio guest had told him that addicts hang out around treatment centers because drugs are so readily available there. He parked on Foothill to watch the house, waiting for a likely prospect to leave. Within minutes, a twenty-five to thirty-year-old muscular white man emerged, long black hair tied in a ponytail, sporting a thick mustache, brass earring dangling from one ear. Paul jumped out of the car and jogged toward him, his loud footsteps causing the man to turn sideways to make room for passing.

"Excuse me," Paul said, pointing to the house, "do you work there?"

"Me. Hell no. You a narc?"

Paul shook his head.

"You trying to buy? I can get any drug you want. Good stuff, good prices."

He had hoped for such an opening. "I need a gun. Also, handcuffs. Can you get them, no questions asked? It's worth five hundred dollars."

The man dragged on a cigarette, showing several missing teeth. "You planning to off someone? You don't look the type. For two grand I'll do it for you?"

"No thanks. Can you get one? Small would be best." The man nodded.

"Could you get bullets that anesthetize but don't kill? I'll pay extra."

"Hey, I'm a mom and pop operation, not a supermarket."

They agreed to meet in the Hofbrau on Broadway at 8:00 that night.

The smell of stale beer reached him from a block away. Broken bottles littered the small parking lot, and a man lay against the wall of the building clutching a bottle. Paul tried to enter the dingy restaurant unobtrusively, but his supplier had arrived first and greeted him like a long-lost friend. "Here," he shouted, waving his arms for emphasis, "over here." As Paul approached, he dropped his voice to a whisper. "The gun's a beauty." He chomped on a mammoth turkey leg, spewing small bits of flesh as he spoke. "But I had to pay premium dollar. It'll cost $800 plus $100 for the cuffs. I couldn't get the bullets you wanted but threw in extra regulars for free."

Having prepared himself for last-minute extortion, Paul carried $1,000. "Let's go out to the parking lot."

The gun had a solid heft. "It's a snub-nosed 38 special. Shoots six rounds, barrel's under three inches, can take a gorilla out at close range." Paul nodded and counted out eight hundred-dollar bills. The East 14th Street store carried the same gun for about $100.

The man repeated his previous offer. "You sure you don't want me to off him. Satisfaction guaranteed. It'll be worth the extra money."

Paul said he meant only to scare somebody. He planned to brandish the gun, and might have shot an anesthetic bullet, but had no intention of shooting regular ones. The man said he'd already loaded the gun. "You wave a gun, you better be prepared to fire." He shoved the extras into Paul's pocket. "Keep 'em, my connection don't give refunds. You can always shoot stray cats." He wrote down a contact name and phone number 'for future services,' and added, "Now don't go getting into no trouble."

Arturo reported that he had successfully delivered the message to Paul. When he told Marice where, she asked him to get his friends to set up surveillance on Paul. She wanted to be contacted immediately when he left the house. She also asked Arturo to get her a gun.

Learning a New Skill

Paul arose at sunrise and drove to the San Leandro Marina. He climbed down to the water's edge and marveled at the seagulls, watching as salty winds whipped toward land and blew them off their flight paths. To him they were undistinguishable except for minor size differences, and he wondered how naturalists like Jane Goodall recognized every member of a large group. A young couple who had camped out overnight and been enjoying the morning interrupted his thoughts. They arose noisily from a blanket under a nearby tree when his intention to stay became clear. Momentarily startled, he called out, "Sorry, I didn't see you, I'll move," but they scurried off rearranging their clothes and soon disappeared out of seeing and hearing range.

The crystalline waters would attract boaters later on, but at 6:00 A.M. the only sounds came from waves crashing against rocks. Paul cocked the gun and aimed at a streak of sunlight on the water. The recoil shook his entire arm and made a shockingly loud noise. A tiny splash broke the surface far from the target. Nervous, he looked around for the couple or other possible observers, but the marina was deserted. Sorry that he hadn't brought cotton to stuff into his ears, he aimed at a nearby tree and squeezed the trigger again. Another bad miss. He decided that his supplier had been right about being prepared to use the gun. He had lots of bullets in his arsenal and began practicing in earnest. By the time the first car approached about an hour later, his accuracy had improved considerably.

Devoted Follower

Sitting in the easy chair, pen and tape recorder at the ready, Paul tried to evaluate his plan against all contingencies. It didn't take him long to conclude that the plan stank—not so much a plan as a bunch of idle wishes—that Brent would be terrified by the gun; that he'd see the error of his evil ways and renounce them; that he'd spend the remainder of his days doing volunteer work in a soup kitchen. Might as well plan to have Marvin, Donna, and his dad return to life.

The doorbell rang. He'd been stupidly sitting near a window with the curtains open. If the visitor were a friend, to ignore the bell would be rude. Hoping for a Jehovah's witness or magazine salesman—anyone who wouldn't require a lengthy interaction—he opened. A person, gray robed and cowled, tossed something at his feet. Paul jumped back and slammed the door. For several seconds he stood motionless, breathing hard. No sounds came from the other side. The person hadn't left. Paul peeked out the window and saw a figure facing the door, kneeling. Hand on doorknob, Paul called out, "Who are you? What do you want?"

"I would be honored if your eminence would bless me. I have journeyed far to be here."

The voice was a man's, vaguely familiar.

"You have the wrong address."

But he cautiously opened the door. The man had strewn rose petals on the ground; some danced in front of Paul in the gentle draft. The man pulled back the cowl and lifted his head. Completely hairless. Paul leaned forward for a closer look, but several moments passed before he recognized the still prostrate man.

"What the hell are you doing, Cody?"

Cody Certner smiled beatifically. "The great wizard asked me to deliver this letter."

Paul read. "Not everybody is as distrustful as that nasty man McCallum. Cody is not acting. He is certain that you are an emissary from the highly advanced civilization of Jorad. The music world may have lost a giant, but I will receive a high score and you have gained a devoted servant."

Denoument

Paul called to say he needed to talk. Brent was agreeable. "Alright old buddy, get your ass over here."

He stuck the loaded gun into a side pocket of his pants and handcuffs into another pocket. Too bulgy, so he shifted them to the rear waistband and pulled a sweatshirt down over his shirt. Breaking into houses had been crazy enough—the gun introduced a whole new level of intensity. He left goodbye notes on the kitchen table for his mother, Marice, and Leonard, and a note for detective Lenz detailing his movements. He intended to retrieve the notes unopened but had to plan for the unexpected.

As soon as Arturo reported that Paul had gotten in his car, Marice asked him to follow and call back with the location. On a hunch, she drove toward the Piedmont address and arrived only minutes after their two-car procession.

Arturo parked down the street. Paul exited the car and stuck gun and handcuffs under his waistband in the back. He walked gingerly down the driveway, hunched over in fear that the cuffs would jingle or the gun discharge and blast through his spine. He intended to cuff Brent at gunpoint, cuff him to Dominic if both were there. Then, search warrant be damned, he would scour the house for incriminating evidence. Though inadmissible in court, the evidence would persuade police to search for something they could use. At the least, it would force Brent to curtail his activities.

Brent seemed slightly tipsy. He clapped his hands to Paul's shoulders and told him to get comfortable. "Dominic's not here, so I'll be your slave. What's your pleasure? What can I get you to drink?

Dominic's absence simplified matters, but Paul suspected that Brent had hidden weapons throughout the house. He asked for a beer. When Brent turned to the kitchen, he lifted a chair cushion and slipped a page of the morning *Tribune* underneath. If he ended up dead, and Brent denied having seen him, his fingerprints would impeach Brent's testimony.

Paul asked, "Have you picked the next victim?" Hand into waistband, he gripped the handle and curled his index finger around the trigger. One swift movement and Brent would have no chance to react.

"Ah, right to business. Glad you've become so dedicated. No, not yet. The next target is still unknown and enjoying his last days of normalcy."

Suddenly, as unexpected as a rainstorm in the Sahara, Brent started to cry. Both hands covering his face, his head began bobbing to some silent rhythm. Stunned, Paul tightened his grip on the gun but kept it hidden. Between heaves of his large chest, Brent lamented the way he mistreated people. He said he'd been a decent person, a devoted husband for eight years and father for four. Then his wife and daughter had been killed in a car crash when a drunken driver veered into their lane and forced them off an embankment. The son of a congressman, the driver had received a five-year suspended sentence. Brent said the killing—"I refuse to call it an accident"—had occurred forty years ago to the day. He had started "Ontological Configurations" soon afterwards with the driver as his first target.

Brent waved his arms and pounded on a coffee table. "There's more wealth in this room than most people make in their lifetime. Without them, meaningless." He slurred the last few words and tripped into a sofa. "Sorry, I don't usually let people see this side of me. Thanks for listening, but you didn't come here to see me blubber. The circus is over, what's on your mind?"

Paul joined him on the sofa. "You're right, I'm here for a reason.

I'm through writing scripts."

For several seconds neither man spoke. Brent took several slow, deep breaths while Paul waited for him to regain composure. At last he said, "You've survived some terrible shit. I'll never forgive you for the murders and what you did to my mother, and if I can scrape up evidence to get you convicted I'll do it. But realistically, that won't happen. You got your revenge. Why continue hurting innocent people? You're wealthy, you can get top-notch therapy, so quit and stay out of prison. Give up your sick game."

Inches apart, they sat eyeball to eyeball. Seconds passed. Brent began sobbing again, hands on cheeks and mouth quivering. Paul loathed the man, yet he empathized. One hand patted Brent's back, the other relaxed its grip.

As abruptly as the crying had started, Brent threw back his head and broke the silence with a roar. "Did you believe that shit about my wife and kids? Damn, I'm good. I can do pathos like nobody's business."

Paul whipped out the gun and shouted, "Don't move." He backed away beyond Brent's reach. Brent didn't move except to twirl his fingers and smirk. Paul fumbled for the handcuffs. Brent said, "Turn around dickhead, a surprise awaits." Keeping the gun pointing squarely at Brent's chest, Paul slowly twisted his neck. Dominic stood in the doorway aiming a rifle at his head.

Brent said, "Did you think I'm too dumb to have security? Dom's always here to guard me, aren't you big boy."

Dominic grunted. Brent said, "You set off my silent metal detector at the front door. My latest script calls for a woman's head to turn up in the target's bed. Using yours will cost me points, but I'll make the sacrifice. Of course, you wrecked my chances at a lifetime performance award."

Marice and Arturo crept up to the window just in time to see Dominic motion Paul to put up his hands.

Brent said, "Too bad Paul, you had the makings of a decent script writer. You might have become famous. Well, maybe posthumously."

One last hope, one skinny straw to grasp. Maybe not so skinny. After all, Brent had just praised his creative abilities. Paul screamed, "You bastard, you don't care who kills who. Does Dominic end up on death row or will he have to duel your next chump writer?"

Dominic blinked. "What's he talking about?" Brent shrugged, unconcerned with Paul's stratagem. He was having fun.

Face contorted, Paul looked directly at Brent but shouted for Dominic's ears. "You said I just had to scare Dominic. I didn't know it was him or me."

Brent cracked his palm against Paul's cheek. Dominic blinked again and swung the gun barrel. Brent growled, "What the hell are you doing?"

"You'd better sit. I need to think."

Now Paul turned to Dominic. "Ask your boss why he had me bring this gun." Gun in hand, he waved expressively.

Dominic leveled the rifle, and both men flinched. "Put down that gun or I'm gonna blow you away." Paul complied. Then all three men started talking at once.

Brent: "Surely you don't believe that shit. You know you're my man, D."

Dominic: "What's he talking about?"

Paul: "C'mon Dominic, open your eyes. Ask him to show you his last script. If I had agreed to kill you, he would have cheered me on."

The two window peepers couldn't hear much but had no trouble grasping the desperateness of Paul's situation. Arturo ran to the cars to snatch up newspapers, maps, owner's manuals, and a paper bag. He rolled up a paper and shoved it down into his just-filled gas tank. They piled the combustibles under the window and added a few dead leaves.

Brent, facing the window, spotted the small fire first. "What the fuck is going on? Dominic, someone's out there. Quick, the gun."

Dominic whirled and saw a plume of smoke. "I'm hanging onto this. You can take his."

Brent grabbed Paul's 38 and rushed to the door. Marice

ducked behind a small tree, Arturo following. Brent fired at the retreating backside, and the bullet found flesh. Arturo screamed in pain. He advanced for the kill, at the same time exposing his own large body. Marice remembered Arturo's teaching—squeeze slowly and be ready for the recoil. Her first shot hit him in the stomach, her second in the chest. Brent fell and started moaning, slowly, softly, almost like a crooner rehearsing notes. Hands clutching stomach, he rolled to one side and tried unsuccessfully to lift his head.

Dominic pulled Paul up by the collar and shoved the gun to his ear. "Move."

They walked outside, Paul in front, Dominic steering. The fire had burnt itself out. Although his left buttocks was searing, Arturo summoned the strength to yell, "Police, throw down your weapons, we've got you surrounded." Dominic pulled Paul back into the house. His right hand pointed the gun, his vise-like left encircled Paul's neck.

Marice followed up on Arturo's lead. She tried to muster an authoritative voice. "Release the hostages and come out with your hands up."

Paul recognized Marice's voice immediately, although her presence baffled him. "Listen Dominic, those aren't cops, they're my friends. Whatever you've done, we don't have any evidence against you and we don't care. Brent must have stashed lots of valuables in this house. Take them and disappear."

"How do I know your pals won't shoot?"

"They just want to get me out safely."

"I hate that fat bastard."

Dominic kept the gun pointed but released his grip and let Paul walk back to the door. Paul called out "Don't shoot. Nobody else will be hurt."

Brent lay a short distance away, eyes open, the front of his once light blue shirt now colored dark brown. Hands on stomach, he tried to staunch the flow of blood.

Marice rose from her hiding place in the bushes. Dominic

swung the gun in her direction, then pointed it toward the ground. As soon as Paul saw her, his facial muscles that had pulled downward for weeks abruptly changed direction. His face became a smile-mask. She leaped into his outspread arms, and he stroked her hair while whispering over and over again, "I love you." The refrain became a duet. Wetness seeped from her eyes and down his shirt. Cupping her face in both hands, tilting it upward, he kissed both streams of tears. "Marice, I've missed you so much."

Dominic lay down his rifle as Arturo limped over. Paul said, "You're the man from the gun store. I think I owe you my life." He asked Marice to take Arturo to a hospital, but Arturo said his doctor cousin Jorge could handle the wound. Marice pointed to Brent, lying only yards away from them, fully conscious, able to hear the conversation. "He needs immediate help. Somebody call for an ambulance." Brent tried to sit up, but blood spurted from his mouth and chest and he fell back moaning.

Paul said, "We'll take care of him, but first you two have to get out of here." Marice drove off with Arturo lying across the back seat on his stomach.

"You said you hate Brent. Why did you work for him?"

"A guy came to the gym where I work out, said he needed some muscle. Easy work, good pay. I'm no altar boy, so I accepted. Beat up a coupla guys who tried to run out on a debt, and got two grand plus a quarter kilo of coke. He introduced me to Brent. I did some errands, not all completely kosher if you know what I mean. The fucker had me followed. He's got tapes with enough evidence to put me away for many years."

"I thought you were buddies."

"He made sure I knew my place. To serve. The fucker loved sending me on errands in the middle of the night."

"Did you think about forcing him to tell you where the tapes are?"

"He warned me he had copies, and if I made him turn over one copy, another would automatically be sent to the cops. I wished I had the guts to kill him, but believe it or not, I'm not a killer."

"Until now."

The rifle lay on the ground, only a few feet away. Paul lunged, but the big man was quicker. Paul cried out, "No Dominic, don't do it."

Dominic pointed the rifle toward Paul. "Stay back." He hovered over Brent's prone form, circled twice, grinned as Brent's eyes gaped upwards trying to follow. He jabbed the rifle until it almost touched Brent's nose, then pulled it back and jabbed again.

Paul inched forward. "Dominic, he's not worth a murder rap. Let's get him to a hospital."

Dominic waved him back. He planted his feet on each side of his former employer's head and shoved the rifle just above the right eye. Then, smiling, he whispered the last words Brent ever heard. "Bye fat boy."

"Did Brent really ask you to off me?"

"You know he loved playing one person against another."

"You didn't answer my question."

"I never owned or even touched a gun until a couple of weeks ago. I bought it because of what Brent demanded. But I never had any intention of shooting you."

"You still didn't—"

"Hey, we'd better start cleaning up. What if a neighbor heard the shots and called the police."

They dragged the body inside and messed up the pristine white carpet. Paul vomited. Dominic made tea to settle his stomach. Surmising that nobody else would visit that night, Paul asked Dominic to give him a second house tour. A room of wall-to-wall videos included hundreds of commercial movies but also three long rows with covers marked in Brent's handwriting. They found a "Paul," a "Marice," and a "Dominic."

Paul said, "No reason to watch. Let's box and burn them. Dominic, even if he's made other copies, you've got nothing to worry about. There must be a fortune in artwork and other things in this house. Take what you can and disappear a rich man."

The room that had once contained apparent spy apparatus held only a chair and a large, locked desk. Dominic shot the desk open. One drawer contained what appeared to be score sheets with initials but no full names. The sheets had notations such as "accomplished in 1 day, + 3" and "T committed suicide, – 5." A second drawer held several large-denomination bills. Paul stuffed the score sheets in his pocket and handed the money to Dominic. Two wall safes disgorged more money. Dominic insisted that his new friend share. He said, "Help me carry the body to the car, and leave the rest to me. I know where to dump it. Maybe in 100 years some scientist will find the bones and think he discovered a missing link."

They vacuumed and mopped the floor, washed away the blood and vomit, and wiped fingerprints from whatever they had touched. They shook hands. Then Dominic stayed to salvage what he could while Paul rushed home to collect and destroy his notes.

End of Oc

Paul told Leonard that the situation with Brent had been resolved and they could be friends again. He asked Leonard to get all the numbers called from Brent's phones during the previous year.

Paul bought a laptop computer for Arturo. He put the rest of his share of the money in a locker at the Oakland airport and sent the key with a printed, unsigned note to the director of the West Oakland Free Clinic. The note explained what the key would open. To ensure that the money would be used properly, he added that copies were being sent to the editors of the *Tribune* and *Montclarion*.

The score sheets listed twenty-six sets of initials, which indicated that the original group of players had increased in number. Paul looked for matches between the initials and Leonard's phone print-outs. He found thirty-three and sent each a message. At least seven recipients must have been baffled.

Ontological Configurations: Part II

A RECENT ALTHOUGH STILL undetected homicide should alert all players (hereafter referred to as Brents) that continued participation in Ontological Configurations would be extremely hazardous. Brents who terminate immediately and forever will not be terminated. You shall be watched.

Bronson Colfax hobbled out to the security gate for the newspaper. On top of the paper, too insubstantial to be holding anything dangerous, was a large envelope bearing his name. He took the envelope inside and slit at the folds. Soon afterwards he dialed his scriptwriter to say "I won't be needing you." Colfax thought, "OC was fun while it lasted, but I'm not sorry. That man was a bully." Then he went inside and lovingly fondled the Hughes. The same theme with minor variations played in the homes of several other billionaires.

PART II

Debriefing and Catharsis

Arturo recovered quickly, Marice did not. "I don't care how despicable he was, how could you stand there and watch him die?" Paul insisted he'd been powerless. Marice said she needed time alone to come to terms with her part. Finally, after a week of twice daily phone calls, she agreed to meet for drinks at Paul's along with Joanna, Leonard, Arturo, and his cousin Jorge. They discussed what had happened, and all agreed that the world without Brent was a better place. Except Marice—she sat next to Joanna, drinking wine, forcing smiles.

When the discussion had run its course, Paul held up an envelope. "I'd like you all to play a game. The winner gets dinner for two at Chez Panisse. Here's the receipt for reservations." He explained how cryptic crossword puzzles work and gave a few examples, then said, "I've constructed cryptic clues for a quote attributed to Robert Browning."

Get possession of teak sculpture. 4 letters
A street in another direction. 4 letters
Romance means nothing in tennis. 4 letters
Also held by Roman deity. 3 letters
Yours and mine together sounds like one of 24. 3 letters
Heart throb on the ground. 5 letters
History holds present to be. 2 letters
In the middle of grave is an article. 1 letter
Atom bomb produces final resting place. 4 letters

He gave everybody a card with the clues and a pad and pencil. They assumed contemplative postures—again except for Marice. She took the materials but just held them. Paul squeezed her shoulders. "Try, honey." Joanna said "C'mon Eece, let's one of us win and take the other to dinner." Jorge called out, "You folks are in trouble. I got two already." Ten minutes later, Leonard grinned and hugged Paul. He said, "That's a wonderful sentiment. I'll take the tickets please."

SOLUTIONS

Get possession of teak sculpture. Make a sculpture of 'teak,' that is, rearrange its letters, to make a 4 letter word that means 'get possession of.' TAKE

A street in another direction. 'A street' means 'a way,' and so does 'in another direction.' AWAY

Romance means nothing in tennis. The word 'love' means both 'romance' and 'nothing' in tennis. LOVE

Also held by Roman deity. The words 'Roman deity' hold the word 'and,' which means 'also.' AND

Yours and mine together sounds like one of 24. Yours and mine together is 'our,' which sounds like 'hour.' OUR

Heart throb on the ground. 'Throb' suggests an anagram of 'heart.' 'Earth' is an anagram and means 'on the ground.' EARTH

History holds present to be. 'History' contains 'is,' which is the present tense of 'to be.' IS

In the middle of grave is an article. The letter 'a,' an article, is in the middle of the word 'grave.' A

Atom bomb produces final resting place. 'Atom bomb' holds 'tomb,' a final resting place. TOMB

Everybody clapped, and Joanna stood up. "That is a wonderful sentiment. We should all show our love with a group hug."

Marice stood too. Then, to nobody's surprise, she started to sob. Loud, heaving sobs, chest convulsing, whole body swaying. Paul and Joanna rushed over, but she backed away. Then she whispered three sentences, just three, but they were terrifying. "You five guys are wonderful, and I love each of you. But I committed a terrible sin and you can't help except by praying for me. I've decided to confess to the police."

Leonard responded first. Eyes narrowed, he said "So, the clean-cut, well-educated, gorgeous white girl's gonna confess. You'll probably get a six month suspended sentence. Extenuating circumstances. But the nigger who withheld vital information about a brutal double murder? I'll die in Quentin."

"Don't worry, I won't implicate you. But if I don't confess they'll find someone else to convict, probably a black man."

Paul swatted Leonard. "She's in a bad way if she can't tell that you're joking." Turning to Marice, "Don't go to the police. You saved my life, but a jury might not believe you. Please, I don't want to lose you again."

She apologized for being such a burden. He said, "You're a hero. If you hadn't shot Brent, Arturo and I would be dead. Who knows how many more people would have become targets."

They persuaded her, but she wrote out a confession and made copies for Paul and Leonard. "If anybody is convicted, I'll turn myself in."

Depression Victim Number Two

Audrey Combes started seeing a widower from her apartment complex. He adored her, and Paul welcomed him into the family. Leonard prospered. His latest novel received glowing pre-publication reviews, and the *Tribune* featured him as a Bay Area literary star. Paul regarded Brent's death as unfortunate but unavoidable and well-deserved. He mourned for Marvin and Donna but finally absolved himself of responsibility for their deaths. Colombo grew fatter.

Marice did not fare well. Self-images constantly change, and hers had undergone many transformations. Depending on company and mood, she had been loving daughter, little sister, big sister, good Catholic, questioning Catholic, apostate, and student. Those aspects were replaced by images of seductress, prostitute, deceiver, and murderer. She had lured one man to his death and fatally shot another. She obsessively replayed every detail and always ended with two bloody, lifeless bodies. Her energy and appetite diminished, and her sensuous figure became almost gaunt. She trusted few people outside of her family and Paul.

Paul tried occupational therapy, telling her that the mugging had left his mother weak and in need of help with household chores. Marice accepted the assignment and, in the presence of Paul's mother, became a great pretender. But pretending took effort and stopped when she was alone.

Nights were especially hard. She and Paul slept together but her libido, at an all-time low, made sex a rarity. Sometimes he curled next to her. Pressing her against him, he crooned, "Hush little baby, don't you cry. Daddy's gonna buy you a mockingbird." Sleep-deprived himself, he kneaded the taut muscles in her shoulders and neck until she fell back limply for another hour or two. Then she'd awaken and, with no distractions in the silent dark, invariably turn her thoughts to Callahan and Brent. They shaped her dreams. She took aspirins daily to relieve headaches, and developed a steady ringing in her ears.

She apologized for being such a burden. He said, "You're a hero. If you hadn't shot Brent, Arturo and I would be dead. Who knows how many more people would have become targets."

Paul told Marice that they could at last get to know each other properly. "Seeing you as Brent's servant girl was the worst moment of my life."

"How could you have thought I liked that man! I just hope he didn't ruin us. After starting with all those lies, we might never enjoy a normal relationship."

"We'll have the greatest relationship since King Kong met Fay Wray. And if we're together because of some demented game, then it's the best game ever invented."

"Maybe you find me attractive only because he conditioned you that way."

"Then he must have conditioned every man on this planet."

"You're certifiable. Don't you ever get depressed?"

"Until recently, only once for more than a day. Senior year in high school, I was voted best student/athlete. Received a scholarship offer from KU and dated the homecoming queen. I was full of myself and probably thoroughly obnoxious. Then I started asking, 'Is this it? Is this the highlight of my existence?' That depressed me for about a week."

"What got you out of it?"

"My favorite teacher turned me on to some philosophy essays. Having grown up with the bible, I was shocked by Bertrand Russell's attacks on religion. So, while many of my friends experimented with drugs and found THE answer, I started doubting all easy answers. But it was exciting. I even wrote a poem. Want to hear it?"

He recited from memory:

Who Am I?
Solipsist, explaining solipsism
Fatalist, rearranging world about him
Leaf in wind, striving to direct its fate
Automaton, switched on to "contemplate"
Hedonist, impelled toward pain
Gentle soul, hands red with blood stain
Somber funeral for I who hoped for circus
Roll of toilet paper, seeking higher purpose.

"You were ancient at eighteen. How did that cheerful ditty improve your mood?"

"The issues made life interesting. That's when I first dreamed about writing a novel."

"Why 'blood stain' and funeral?"

"My dog got run over because of my carelessness. Maybe I had some hint of the future and the words foreshadowed."

"Your insistence on trying to make sense of everything is what attracts me to you the most."

"Why do malcontents attract you?"

Marice said she'd led a sheltered childhood. "I grew up thinking I had a contract with God. Be good and He'd protect me against all suffering." Her parents and the sisters in school encouraged her to believe that faith protects against misfortune. "What a joke. Right after I turned fourteen we learned that my baby brother had leukemia. He died a year later. My parents' faith got them through it fairly well, but it tore me up. Not long after, three boys I knew offered me a ride home from the library. They raped me."

She fought not to cry. "Adversity strengthens some people, but I got weaker. I tried holding onto Catholicism for my parents' sake, but it no longer made sense. I couldn't love a God who allowed such cruelty. Sometimes I sat for hours on my living room floor, not wanting to move and face the world. I stopped loving God but needed Him. I still need something to fill the void. You give me hope."

She blew her nose. "It's unfair to impose my misery on others. I want people to see funny, cheerful Marice."

Paul stopped dispensing tissues and took a few for himself. He rubbed his eyes. "You're right to be unhappy. I'm so lucky to have you, but poor you, you're stuck with me."

They bought bicycles and explored the Tilden Park trails every Saturday, extending the distance each week. Leonard and Joanna occasionally accompanied them. As her physical condition improved, so did her mood. On one outing, the quartet left their bikes and set off on a walking trail. The two men plowed ahead like army recruits on a basic training march, while the women pivoted their heads constantly from side to side. Halfway up a dry, rocky hill Joanna shouted, "Look over there, those flowers are gorgeous." The sisters skipped toward the small stand, excitedly calling to the men. Marice said, "They're called golden blazing stars. Have you ever seen anything so pretty?"

The men had hiked the trails many times and never noticed. Later, in what they thought was a patch of weeds, Joanna said, "Smell this mugwort. Herbalists say that a mugwort sachet hung over your bed will make your dreams more interesting."

Paul whispered to Marice, "My waking life is better than dreams ever were."

Joanna inhaled deeply. "Isn't the air invigorating. On hot days like today, the pines pump out tons of resin. I love it."

They filled their lungs and approved the smell, then resumed walking and came to a meadow of wildflowers. The women dropped to their knees for close inspection. Joanna spotted a large madrone, its deep red bark contrasting splendidly with the nearby ferns. "Madrones are notoriously slow growers. I've never seen such a big one."

Paul stretched out his arms and beckoned his companions to approach for hugs. Gesturing expansively at their surroundings, he stammered, "This. You three. I'm blessed." Eight eyes teared up until Leonard shouted, "The boy is positively beatific. And as articulate as ever." Marice beamed. She too felt blessed.

Weaving

Three years earlier, Marice had driven to Stockton to meet an eighty-year-old man famous for crafting looms. By day's end she'd ordered a four-harness collapsible loom, and when it arrived three months later weaving became an important part of her daily routine. Before long, all her family had an original Marice Soriano. She'd left the loom in her parents' home when she moved to an apartment. Paul asked her to move in with him when her lease expired. With the money saved, she rented a large studio less than a mile from the College of Arts and Crafts and installed the loom.

She advertised for others to share space and found two students—another weaver and a painter. Once settled in, they encouraged visitors. With Peet's coffee brewing and music in the background, the studio became a popular hangout for the local art crowd. Artists with sketchpads sat staring out the window hoping to see interesting passersby. Students and occasional faculty dropped in to socialize. She let them display their creations wherever they found empty space.

Her first weavings were symmetrical ties and placemats. Then, as her confidence grew, she tried larger pieces with intricate patterns. For Paul's birthday, she wove a six-foot by four-foot tapestry showing brown sands merging with blue waters under a rising orange sun. He hung it in their bedroom and called it, next to her, his most treasured possession.

"Shut Up"

They made love several times that night. More accurately, they had several orgasms—the lovemaking continued nonstop. Paul quoted Nietzsche: "Poets act shamelessly toward their experiences: they exploit them." He said, "If I'm ever successful as a writer it will be because of you. You're giving me all my great experiences." She said, swinging a leg over his and smiling giddily, "Shut up."

OC

Paul hadn't yet read everything in the packet that "Colonel" Venn had given him. They read together and verified the accuracy of several items.

In 1947, the Crown Prince of Saudi Arabia came by enormous limousine to the doors of a luxurious Hollywood restaurant. Once seated, he requested a particular song from the band. When they finished he opened a pouch and removed a magnificent jewel. His servant presented the jewel to the bandleader as the celebrity-filled audience looked on dumbfounded. Upon leaving, the Crown Prince scattered the jewels from his pouch on the floor. The guests scrambled madly for them, unaware that the "Crown Prince" was in reality jokester Jim Moran. He had bought the jewels in a dime store.

Dr. James Phillips practiced medicine for thirty-four years throughout the south and southwest. He diagnosed, dispensed medicines, and performed surgeries. During the course of a routine damage suit arising out of a collision between Dr. Phillips' car and a truck, the opposition attorney made inquiries. He learned that "Doc" Phillips' only degree came from a Penn State correspondence course in butter making and technology of milk.

News clipping from the Oakland Tribune, 6/20/88: After a six-month investigation into health care and the licensing of physicians, a congressional subcommittee reported that law enforcement agencies suspect that 10,000 people in the United States possess fraudulent medical degrees. Many people posing as doctors never even graduated from high school.

In Oxford, California, Bessie Mount opened a house of prostitution that catered only to the elite. She became a valued member of the community, liked by women as well as men and famous for her sumptuous dinner parties. During World War II, while doing Red Cross work, she met and later married a handsome soldier. Twenty years after she'd started in Oxford, military police raided her house and demanded that all the women, Bessie included, submit to medical examinations. She refused but they overpowered her—and found out she was a man.

A study published in American Scientist magazine showed that forty-three percent of students and fifty percent of faculty members claimed direct knowledge of misconduct in their laboratories, including faking of results.

Late Night Radio

Paul asked to switch his radio time-slot to late night. On successive nights, he hosted a philosopher who had just published a solution to a baffling logical paradox; the mother of a Cambodian teenager who had died in police custody; and a roundtable of two newspaper editors, two reporters, an attorney, and a judge who debated First Amendment rights. The philosopher, the mother, and two of the roundtable contacted Arlene to praise Paul. They mentioned his preparededness, sense of humor, and ability to clarify complex issues. Ratings soared, and the executive vice-president of local television channel 2 invited him to develop a prospectus for a TV show. He declined out of loyalty to Arlene.

Marice's world had expanded, and her determination to test and extend boundaries made Paul's life at the station unpredictably exciting. He interviewed guests in a comfortable room while a security guard and technician, the only other people in the building at the late hour, worked elsewhere. The security guard had been introduced to Marice and instructed to let her in. Though Paul was his buddy, he was delighted to conspire with her.

One night's schedule included a debate between the vice-president of "Mothers Against Pornography" and a woman from the Libertarian Party. When Marice read the guest list, she knew it was time to act. As she'd anticipated, the Mother Against and the Libertarian began insulting each other and issuing physical threats within minutes of the introductions. Paul tried unsuccessfully to keep them civil. His break for a commercial cued Marice's entrance.

She appeared in the doorway with arms akimbo, statuesque in four-inch heels, like the avatar of a vengeful goddess. Metal bracelets dangled from her wrists and ankles, a chain hung from her waist, and she crackled a whip in their general direction. Aside from the shoes and jewelry, she stood naked. She waggled her tongue at Paul while intoning in a bored, nasal voice, "Theresa has the flu, so the agency sent me tonight. Will you be done soon? I've got two other calls."

The eyes of the "Mother Against…" bulged like those of a diver hauled rapidly from 1,000 fathoms deep. Fighting for composure, Paul announced that an intruder had entered the studio and caused a momentary but harmless disruption. The Libertarian cackled while her rival stormed out screaming that she would sue.

During the drive home, Paul said in a pretend-grieved voice, "You're not interested enough in me as a person. All you care about is sex." Marice bit his earlobe and said, "Look who's talking. You'd probably be just as happy if I was an inflatable doll." The corners of her mouth crinkled slightly at the thought.

OC

Scientific findings originate with individuals or small groups who often have reason to conceal them. Ninety percent of scientists who ever lived are alive today, ninety percent of the scientific literature has been written by scientists now alive, and more than ninety percent of research money for science has been spent in the last generation. Since 1660, when the Royal Society was founded in England, the total size of science has increased about a millionfold. An implication is that for every major discovery made in 1665, about a million should be made each current year. Yet the number of major discoveries per century has remained fairly constant. Historian Robert Root-Bernstein concluded that today's scientists aren't trained properly. A more provocative conclusion is that revolutionary discoveries are being made at the seventeenth century pace and kept secret.

Imagine a scientist who discovered that a readily available chemical, taken in the right dose, reverses aging. Going public would be disastrous, because nobody would die and births would continue until all habitable space was used up. Other discoveries that would be shared only with family and close friends include devices for time travel and mind.

Psychologists estimate that Einstein's IQ was about 180. According to the probability distribution of the normal curve, an intelligence of his magnitude occurs only once in ten million births. Extremely rare. On the other hand, the population of the earth is seven billion. Probably about 700 people with Einsteinian IQs are alive today. Strange that we haven't heard of them.

Idiot Savant

Marice phoned Paul to pick her up from a friend's house, and he covered a whole sheet of paper writing the complicated directions. On the ride home, she poked his ribs. "If I'd been directing Linda, I'd have told her to drive to the house with the topiary in front, make a left, and go 100 yards."

"So?"

"So, you can define 'topiary' and have driven past that house dozens of times, but I'll bet those directions wouldn't have meant a thing."

She was right, he'd seen the house without seeing it. A UC physiology professor had told Paul's radio audience about a study in which experimenters placed electrodes in individual cells within the auditory system of cats, then exposed the cats to various sounds. The electrodes picked up strong activity. Next, the experimenters pumped fish odors into the room, and the auditory responses virtually disappeared. The cats had literally stopped hearing the clicks. Paul mused that his own senses had atrophied and become unresponsive until Marice, by delighting in music, fragrances, textures, and shapes, had resuscitated them.

Paul usually listened to KJAZ while washing the dinner dishes. A few days after the topiary comment the disc jockey played Morgana King singing "A Taste of Honey." He dropped the dishtowel and asked Marice to dance. They danced to Morgana, then to Billie Holiday, then to Mel Torme. When the station cut to a commercial, he teased her about getting her hair cut short.

She feigned anger. "I'm surprised you noticed. You're an idiot savant."

"What?"

"They're the retarded ones with a unique skill like doing lengthy calculations in their heads or reproducing complex musical pieces after a single hearing."

"I know what an idiot savant is."

"Well, you and some of your Mensa-type friends—not Leonard or Gordy—have a special skill, doing well on IQ tests. But the others I've met are idiots about everything else."

She ground her pelvis into his to show she was teasing. But he scowled and tickled her till she screamed for mercy. From that day on, she called him her idiot savant—sometimes idiot for short.

Tour Bus

The guests had left and he sat alone in the studio talking with phone callers during the last half-hour segment. With about ten minutes to go, Marice appeared in the doorway holding a sign: "TAKE OFF YOUR CLOTHES. LET'S START MAKING LOVE JUST BEFORE YOU GO OFF THE AIR." She pulled her shirt over her head, causing Paul to gulp in mid-sentence. Her daring and creativity constantly surprised him, and he loved it. Literally ripping off his tee-shirt, he unbuttoned his pants and dropped everything in a pile, all the while arguing with a caller about the use of animals in scientific research. She rushed in to scoop up the clothes and then retreated beyond the microphone's reach. A moment later she reappeared with a bicycle pump and inflatable doll that soon took the shape of a naked woman. With five minutes left of air time and the caller raging about Paul's callousness, he jammed a ballpoint pen into his thigh to keep from laughing. She pushed the doll within his reach. "Two can play at this game," he thought, and put it on his lap. Constrained by being on the air, he stroked the rubber surface and tried to pantomime ecstasy. Marice smiled and removed her bra, then wriggled seductively out of her pants. Paul pretended not to notice. He kissed the doll but couldn't avert his eyes from her. The pretense became impossible as his penis grew.

She winked and retreated out of sight. Paul, nakedly erect, clutched the doll and watched the second hand revolve with maddening slowness toward twelve. Fifteen, fourteen, thirteen seconds to heaven. Then the elevator door clanked open and he heard a cacophony of voices. Leonard emerged first, in full Salvation Army captain's regalia, followed by an elevator-load of tourists. Paul heard him say, "Many radio personalities work alone. The job may seem glamorous, but it must get boring. Today we can ask famous talk show host Paul Combes how he gets through the lonely nights."

They shared drinks at a nearby bar, during which time Paul said he intended to cut them out of his will. Leonard said goodnight, and the other two went home leaving the doll, unneeded, in the car.

Cryptic Love

Paul and Marice scrutinized the classifieds for a house. They eventually hired a realtor, and after taking them on a whirlwind open house tour, he found a ranch style fixer-upper with a full acre of garden space and a great canyon view. Marice loved it and Paul, relieved not to have to walk into any more strange bedrooms, paid the full asking price and signed purchase papers the same day. The house needed lots of work. With Beatles tapes rocking in the background, sometimes with help from Leonard and Joanna, Paul and Marice sanded and buffed the hardwood floors and painted most of the interior. The move two months later took only a few hours, as Marice insisted they donate all Paul's furnishings to the Salvation Army. She bought a second loom and converted a bedroom to a studio. She asked Paul's mother to live with them, but Audrey Combes refused to intrude.

They bought two cryptic crossword puzzle books, and the puzzles became a nightly diversion. They solved separately at first, until he asked her help one night and permanently altered the process. She reflected on "unconscious lying (8)," then snapped her fingers and said, "Got it. Sleeping." When he began unbuttoning his shirt, she immediately understood. "So, you want to play 'strip cryptic'. I hope your underwear is clean."

They took turns, two minutes maximum per clue. Each failure to solve within the time limit required the removal of one article of clothing. They kissed to make the rules legal and binding.

Formerly pensive, dear (9).

Paul missed and unzipped his fly, but Marice protested. "Hey, you lost, I decide what comes off. I don't want to see that body till it's absolutely necessary. Shoe, please."

expensive

Paul gyrated his hips while removing a shoe and fell clumsily onto the bed. Marice jumped in next to him and they lost several valuable minutes of playing time.

Mediate, bury, and relinquish (9).

Marice missed and pulled the tank top over her head. Paul said, "Uh, uh, I choose. Pants please. Mine." She worked with special diligence at the zipper area. Paul said, "I love word games."

intercede

Gadget for sizing up the king (5).

Paul accused Marice of deliberately missing. She pleaded the fifth and removed her bra.

ruler

Infringes on very French tickets (10).

The difficult clue demanded Paul's total attention. Marice cheated. Standing topless, legs slightly parted, she rolled her tongue slowly across her lips. With one arm resting under her firm breasts and pushing them toward him, she used her free hand to trace lazy circles around her nipples. He closed his eyes to concentrate. She rubbed her chest against his partly hidden forehead. He failed to solve the clue. Soon he was naked. Soon they both were.

trespasses

In the next phase, loser had to do winner's bidding.

It's hard to understand how beast of burden holds up procession prematurely (7).

Marice missed and waited for his command. "This will be an oral task."

She nodded compliantly, and Paul handed her a small box.

"Your task is to say the following—." He drew out the words slowly and deliberately. "Yes Paul, I will marry you."

She threw her arms around him and pulled him onto the bed, then rolled over and straddled him. Bending her head to his ear, she whispered, "Yes Paul, my love, I will marry you." They sat up, and he placed the golden band on her finger.

Paradox.

On a moonlit Saturday night in September, Paul and Marice married on the lawn area outside the Berkeley Men's Faculty Club. Leonard served as best man and Joanna as maid-of-honor. The bridesmaids each wore a Marice-woven sash, the groom's men a Marice-woven tie. Marice's relatives comprised most of the wedding party. Paul's family guests included his mother, Aunt Ida, and two cousins from Kansas.

A few kids zooming down the nearby walkways on skateboards briefly interrupted the ceremony. Then, just as bride and groom prepared to say their final vows, the campanile rang its hourly tune. While waiting for the final ring, Paul said, "This gives you time to change your mind."

Marice slapped his wrist. "I've got you now, there's no escape."

While the wedding party laughed, Paul whispered, "I'm such a lucky man." Marice wholeheartedly agreed.

Dinner followed the reception, with Leonard joining Joanna and other relatives at the main table. When the time came for goodbyes, Paul asked Joanna to give him a minute alone with his best man.

"Leonard, you've been great. Your friendship means an awful lot to me."

Leonard whispered, "By the way, I hope your tuxedo isn't rented—if Joanna says yes, you'll need it again soon."

Paul scowled. "Damn, show these black folk a little kindness and they want to marry your sister-in-law."

Leonard punched his arm, glad to see his friend so happy. After a one-week honeymoon in Kauai, Paul and Marice returned to their now glorious existence.

She whispered, "Yes, Paul, my love, I will marry you." They sat up, and he placed the golden band on her finger.

"Paradox."

On a balmy Saturday night in September, Paul and Maurice married on the lawn area outside the Berkeley Men's Faculty Club. Leonard served as best man and Joanne as maid-of-honor. The bridesmaids each wore [illegible] and Maurice wore [illegible] the grooms [illegible]. Maurice's relatives comprised most of the wedding party. Paul's family guests included his mother, Aunt [illegible], and two cousins from Kansas.

As [illegible] came down the nearby walkway [illegible], Paul [illegible] interrupted the ceremony. They [illegible] just [illegible] and [illegible] prepared [illegible] their [illegible] vows, the [illegible] ring [illegible]. While waiting for the [illegible] ring, Paul said, "[illegible] you [illegible] your mind."

Maurice [illegible], "[illegible] you [illegible]."

All the wedding party laughed. Paul whispered, "I'm such a [illegible] man." Maurice [illegible] agreed.

Dinner followed the reception, with Leonard joining Joanne and other relatives at the main table. When the time came for goodbyes, Paul asked Joanne to give him a minute alone with his best man.

"[illegible] you've [illegible] great. Your [illegible] seemed [illegible]."

Leonard whispered, "By the way, I hope your tuxedo isn't rented [illegible], you'll need it again soon."

Paul [illegible], "[illegible] a little kindness [illegible] to carry you [illegible]."

Leonard [illegible] grin, glad to [illegible] his friend so happy. After a [illegible] honeymoon in Kauai, Paul and Maurice returned to their [illegible] glorious existence.

PART III

End of Interregnum

The happy couple volunteered on a project to deliver surplus restaurant food to shelters for the homeless. The work buoyed their spirits as much as it helped the recipients. They ate well, slept peacefully through most nights, and had wonderful sex. They bought a kiln, and Paul made a set of cups that he insisted on using whenever they had guests. They took singing lessons. For both of them, life had gone from "Which would be easier, pills, gas, or gun?" to "wouldn't trade with anybody." Then, on a quiet Tuesday morning, Paul returned from work to find in their mailbox an ordinary white envelope with no return address. Inside, was a 3 x 5 card.

SURPRISE!

Consider an analogy: A lifelong desert dweller, a Kalahari bushman, is shown an olympic-sized swimming pool. After his initial shock, he'd realize that water is vastly more abundant than he'd thought. Yet his new worldview would still be orders of magnitude from the truth.

Your belief that the world works pretty much the way you think was shaken by your involvement with Brent Willerman. Brent did some clever things. Imagine what an Einstein could do. Consider yourself a bushman and Brent a swimming pool.

OC preceded Brent and still lives on. He was a

target too. The goal of our game is sometimes to accumulate the greatest number of targets. The best players use a "Typhoid Mary" strategy.

Swami Maujgiri Maharaj stood continuously for more than seventeen years between 1955 and 1973. He slept leaning against a pole.

In the 1980s, Melissa Saunders lived for 516 days in a six-feet by seven-feet shack at the top of a pole.

In May, 1986, Ken Own lay on a bed of nails for 300 hours including 132 hours and thirty minutes without a break.

From 1921 to 1954, Simon Rodia built the Watts Towers. He used salvaged steel rods, bed frames, and cement for the framework; and glass bottle fragments, ceramic tiles, and seashells for the thick surface that looks like coral. The central tower is 107 feet high.

Over a two-week period in 1978, eighty-four women in a Singapore television assembly plant began screaming, fainting, committing violent acts, and falling into trance states. Doctors found no physical or psychological causes, and tranquilizers did not help.

In 1975, 144 workers in a southeastern U.S. manufacturing plant suddenly complained of dizziness, nausea, breathing difficulty, and headaches. There was no obvious cause.

In a London teaching hospital in 1973, 102 nurses suddenly complained of headaches, nausea, dizziness, and palpitations. There was no obvious cause.

In 1974, in a southern U.S. shoe manufacturing plant, 121 workers reported headaches, sleepiness, weakness, and dizziness. No obvious cause.

In 1967, 2.3 million ouija boards were sold.

Throughout 1939, U.S. college students competed

to see who could swallow the most live goldfish. The winner swallowed 210. In 1973, the nouvelle cuisine was ground up light bulbs. In a 1987 contest, a Holy Cross student vomited into another's mouth

In 1959, twenty-two women crammed into a telephone booth in Memphis. Others stuffed themselves into volkswagons.

In 1952, 30 million kids wore propellor-topped beanies.

Streaking began in earnest in 1974. The University of Georgia set the record for most streakers at one time, 1,543.

One of the richest men in northern California earned his fortune by inventing the pet rock.

Be advised, solve the next cryptics at your peril. But think hard before you do. We have tools for tracing every reader of this page. If you need answers, write to fredlvtt@gmail.com.

Is the law a reason to keep knowledgeable. Yes (5)

Pitch gets what people aim for. (7)

Now gift is here. (7)

Miserable tears get the very best. (8)

Takes exception to changes holding reversed extension. (10)

Crossword mavens are tragic lovers going from Maine to Florida. (7)

Ego of damsel fair. (4)

Pick the French in splinter group. (6)

And that's how the story ends.

www.ingramcontent.com/pod-product-compliance
Lightning Source LLC
LaVergne TN
LVHW030920080826
845145LV00013B/2976

* 9 7 8 1 9 4 8 5 9 8 5 3 8 *